DREAMLAND

JULIE M. LIPPMANN

Dreamland

Julie M. Lippmann

© 1st World Library – Literary Society, 2005
PO Box 2211
Fairfield, IA 52556
www.1stworldlibrary.org
First Edition

LCCN: 2006902754

Softcover ISBN: 1-4218-1884-1
Hardcover ISBN: 1-4218-1784-5
eBook ISBN: 1-4218-1984-8

Purchase *"Dreamland"*
as a traditional bound book at:
www.1stWorldLibrary.org/purchase.asp?ISBN=1-4218-1884-1

1st World Library Literary Society is a nonprofit
organization dedicated to promoting literacy by:

- Creating a free internet library accessible from any
computer worldwide.
- Hosting writing competitions and offering book
publishing scholarships.

**Readers interested in supporting literacy
through sponsorship, donations or
membership please contact:
literacy@1stworldlibrary.org
Check us out at: www.1stworldlibrary.ORG
and start downloading free ebooks today.**

Dreamland
contributed by Tim, Ed & Rodney
in support of
1st World Library Literary Society

TO

LULU AND MARIE

CONTENTS

THE WAKING SOUL

Larry lay under the trees upon the soft, green grass, with his hat tilted far forward over his eyes and his grimy hands clasped together beneath his head, wishing with all his might first one thing and then another, but always that it was not so warm.

When the children had gone to school in the morning, they had seen Larry's figure, as they passed along the street, stretched out full-length beneath the trees near the gutter curbstone; and when they returned, there he was still. They looked at him with curiosity; and some of the boys even paused beside him and bent over to see if he were sunstruck. He let them talk about him and discuss him and wonder at him as they would, never stirring, and scarcely daring to breathe, lest they be induced to stay and question him. He wanted to be alone. He wanted to lie lazily under the trees, and watch the sunbeams as they flirted with the leaves, and hear the birds gossip with one another, and feel the breeze as it touched his hot temples and soothed him with its soft caresses.

Across the street, upon some one's fence-rail, climbed a honeysuckle vine; and every now and then Larry caught a whiff of a faint perfume as the breeze flitted by. He wished the breeze would carry heavier loads of it and come oftener. It was tantalizing to get just one breath and no more in this way.

But then, that was always the case with Larry; he seemed to get a hint of so many things, and no more than that of any. Often when he was lying as he was now, under green trees, beneath blue skies, he would see the most beautiful pictures before his eyes. Sometimes they were the clouds that drew them for him, and sometimes the trees. He would, perhaps, be feeling particularly forlorn and tired, and would fling himself down to rest, and then in a moment - just for all the world as though the skies were sorry for him and wanted to help him forget his troubles - he would see the white drifts overhead shift and change, and there would be the vision of a magnificent man larger and more beautiful than any mortal; and then Larry would hold his breath in ecstasy, while the man's face grew graver and darker, and his strong arm seemed to lift and beckon to something from afar, and then from out a great stack of clouds would break one milk-white one which, when Larry looked closer, would prove to be a colossal steed; and in an instant, in the most remarkable way, the form of the man would be mounted upon the back of the courser and then would be speeding off toward the west. And then Larry would lose sight of them, just at the very moment when he would have given worlds to see more; for by this time the skies would have grown black, perhaps, and down would come the rain in perfect torrents, sending Larry to his feet and scuttling off into somebody's area-way for shelter. And there he would crouch and think about his vision, fancying to himself his great warrior doing battle with the sea; the sea lashing up its wave-horses till they rose high upon their haunches, their gray backs curving outward, their foamy manes a-quiver, their white forelegs madly pawing the air, till with a

Julie M. Lippmann

wild whinny they would plunge headlong upon the beach, to be pierced by the thousand rain-arrows the cloud-god sent swirling down from above, and sink backward faint and trembling to be overtaken and trampled out of sight by the next frenzied column behind.

Oh! it sent Larry's blood tingling through his veins to see it all so plainly; and he did not feel the chill of his wet rags about him, nor the clutch of hunger in his poor, empty stomach, when the Spirit of the Storm rode out, before his very eyes, to wage his mighty war. And then at other times it would all be quite different, and he would see the figures of beautiful maidens in gossamer garments, and they would seem to be at play, flinging flecks of sunlight this way and that, or winding and unwinding their flaky veils to fling them saucily across the face of the sun.

But none of these wondrous visions lasted. They remained long enough to wake in Larry's heart a great longing for more, and then they would disappear and he would be all the lonelier for the lack of them. That was the greatest of his discouragements. What would he care for heat or cold or hunger or thirst if he could only capture these fleeting pictures once for all, so that he could always gaze at them and dream over them and make them his forever!

That was one of the things for which Larry was wishing as he lay under the trees that summer day. He was thinking: "If there was *only* some way of getting them down from there! It seems to me I 'd do anything in the world to be able to get them down from there. I -"

"No, you would n't," said a low voice next his ear, - "no, you would n't. You 'd lie here and wish and wonder all day long, but you would n't take the first step to bring your pictures down from heaven."

For a moment Larry was so mightily surprised that he found himself quite at a loss for words, for there was no one near to be seen who could possibly have addressed him; but presently he gained voice to say, -

"Oh, I know I could n't get 'em o' course. Folks can't reach up and bring clouds down out o' de sky."

"I did n't say anything about clouds nor about the sky," returned the voice. "I was speaking about pictures and heaven. Folks can reach up and bring pictures down out of heaven. It's done every day. Geniuses do it."

"Who is geniuses?" asked untaught Larry.

"People who can get near enough heaven to catch glimpses of its wonderful beauty and paint it on canvas or carve it in marble for the world to see, or who hear snatches of its music and set them upon paper for the world to hear; and they are called artists and sculptors and composers and poets."

"What takes 'em up to heaven?" queried Larry.

"Inspiration," answered the voice.

"I don't know o' that. I never seen it," the boy returned. "Is it death?"

"No; it is life. But you would n't understand if I could explain it, which I cannot. No one understands it. But it is there just the same. You have it, but you do not know how to use it yet. You never will unless you do something besides lie beneath the trees and dream. Why can't you do something?"

"Oh, I'm tired with all the things I 'm not doin'!" said Larry, in his petulant, whimsical way.

For a little the voice was silent, and Larry was beginning to fear it had fled and deserted him like all the rest; when it spoke again, in its low-toned murmur, like the breath of a breeze, and said, -

"It is cruel to make a good wish and then leave it to wander about the world weak and struggling; always trying to be fulfilled and never succeeding because it is not given strength enough. It makes a nameless want in the world, and people's hearts ache for it and long to be satisfied. They somehow feel there is somewhere a blessing that might be blesseder, a beauty that should be more beautiful. It is then that the little unfledged wish is near, and they feel its longing to be made complete, - to be given wings and power to rise to heaven. Yes; one ought not to make a good wish and let it go, - not to perish (for nothing is lost in this world), but to be unfulfilled forever. One ought to strengthen it day by day until it changes from a wish to an endeavor, and then day by day from an endeavor to an achievement, and then the world is better for it and glad of it, and its record goes above. If all the people who wish to do wonderful things did them, how blessed it would be! If all the people who wish to be good were good, ah, then there would be no more disappointment nor tears nor heartache in the world!"

Larry pondered an instant after the voice had ceased,

and then said slowly: "I *kind* o' think I know what you mean. You think I 'd ought to be workin'. But what could I do? There ain't nothin' I could be doin'."

"Did n't I hear you complaining of me a little while ago, because I did not carry heavy enough loads of honeysuckle scent and did not come often enough? I carried all I was able to bear, for I am not very strong nowadays, and I came as often as I could. In fact, I did my best the first thing that came to hand. I want you to do the same. That is duty. I don't bear malice toward you because you were dissatisfied with me. You did not know. If you tried the best you could and people complained, you ought not to let their discontent discourage you. I brought you a whiff of perfume; you can bring some one a sincere effort. By and by, when I am stronger and can blow good gales and send the great ships safely into port and waft to land the fragrant smell of their spicy cargo, you may be doing some greater work and giving the world something it has been waiting for."

"The world don't wait for things," said Larry. "It goes right on; it does n't care. I 'm hungry and ragged, and I have n't no place to sleep; but the world ain't a-waitin' fer me ter get things ter eat, ner clo'es to me back, ner a soft bed. It ain't a-waiting fer nothin', as I can see."

"It does not stand still," replied the voice; "but it is waiting, nevertheless. If you are expecting a dear, dear person - your mother, for instance -"

"I ain't got no mother," interrupted Larry, with a sorrowful sigh; "she died."

"Well, then - your sister," suggested the voice.

Julie M. Lippmann

"I ain't got no sister. I ain't got nobody. I 'm all by meself," insisted the boy.

"Then suppose, for years and years you have been dreaming of a friend who is to fill your world with beauty as no one else could do, - who among all others in the world will be the only one who could show you how fair life is. While you would not stand still and do nothing what time you were watching for her coming, you would be always waiting for her, and when she was there you would be glad. That is how the world feels about its geniuses, - those whom it needs to make it more wonderful and great. It is waiting for you. Don't disappoint it. It would make you sad unto death if the friend of whom you had dreamed should not come at last, would it not?"

Larry nodded his head in assent. "Does it always know 'em?" he asked. "I mean does the world always be sure when the person comes, it 's the one it dreamed of? Mebbe I'd be dreamin' of some one who was beautiful, and mebbe the real one would n't look like what I thought, and I 'd let her go by."

"Ah, little Lawrence, the world has failed so too. It has let its beloved ones go by; and then, when it was too late, it has called after them in pleading to return. They never come back, but the world keeps repeating their names forever. That is its punishment and their fame."

"What does it need me for?" asked Larry.

"It needs you to paint for it the pictures you see amid the clouds and on the earth."

"Can't they see 'em?" queried the boy.

"No, not as you can. Their sight is not clear enough. God wants them to know of it, and so He sends them you to make it plain to them. It is as though you went to a foreign country where the people's speech was strange to you. You could not know their meaning unless some one who understood their language and yours translated it for you. He would be the only one who could make their meaning clear to you. He would be an interpreter."

"How am I to get that thing you spoke about that 'd take me up to heaven, so's I could bring down the beautiful things I see?" inquired Larry. "Where is it?"

"Inspiration?" asked the voice. "That is everywhere, - all about you, within and without you. You have only to pray to be given sight clear enough to see it and power to use it. But now I must leave you. I have given you my message; give the world yours. Good-by, Lawrence, good-by;" and the voice had ceased.

Larry stretched out his hands and cried, "Come back, oh, come back!"

But the echo of his own words was all he heard in response. He lay quite motionless and still for some time after that, thinking about all the voice had said to him, and when finally he pushed his hat back from before his eyes, he saw the starlit sky smiling down upon him benignantly. And then, from behind a dark cloud he saw the radiant moon appear, and it seemed to him like the most beautiful woman's face he could imagine, peering out from the shadow of her own dusky hair to welcome the night.

He got upon his feet as well as he could, for he was

very stiff with lying so long, and stumbled on toward some dark nook or cranny where he could huddle unseen until the morning; his head full of plans for the morrow, and his heart beating high with courage and hope.

He would dream no more, but labor. He would work at the first thing that came to hand, and then, perhaps, that wonderful thing which the voice had called inspiration would come to him, and he would be able to mount to heaven on it and bring down to earth some of the glorious things he saw. He thought inspiration must be some sort of a magical ladder, that was invisible to all but those given special sight to see and power to use it. If he ever caught a glimpse of it he intended to take hold at once and climb straight up to the blessed regions above; and dreaming of all he would see there, he fell asleep.

In the morning he was awake bright and early, and stretching himself with a long-drawn yawn, set out to find some way of procuring for himself a breakfast. First at one shop-door and then at another he stopped, popping in his shaggy head and asking the man inside, "Give me a job, Mister?" and being in reply promptly invited to "clear out!"

But it took more than this to discourage Larry, heartened as he was by the remembrance of his visions of the day before; and on and on he went, until, at last, in answer to his question - and just as he was about to withdraw his head from the door of the express-office into which he had popped it a moment before - he was bidden to say what it was he could do. Almost too surprised at the change in greeting to be able to reply, he stumbled back into the place and stood a moment in rather stupid silence before his questioner.

"Well, ain't yer got no tongue in yer head, young feller? Seemed ter have a minute ago. Ef yer can't speak up no better 'n this, yer ain't the boy fer us."

But by this time Larry had recovered himself sufficiently to blurt out: "I kin lift an' haul an' run errants an' do all sorts o' work about the place. Won't ye try me, Mister? Lemme carry out that box ter show ye how strong I am;" and suiting the action to the words, he shouldered a heavy packing-case and was out upon the sidewalk and depositing it upon a wagon, already piled with trunks and luggage, before the man had time to reply.

When he returned to the door-step he was greeted with the grateful intelligence that he might stay a bit and see how he got along as an errand-boy if he liked; and, of course, *liking*, he started in at once upon his new office.

That was the beginning. It gave him occupation and, food, but scarcely more than that at first. He had no time for dreaming now, but often when he had a brief moment to himself would take out of his pocket the piece of chalk with which he marked the trunks he carried, and sketch with it upon some rough box-lid or other the picture of a face or form which he saw in his fancy; so that after a time he was known among the men as "the artist feller," and grew to have quite a little reputation among them.

How the rest came about even Larry himself found it hard to tell. But by and by he was drawing with pencil and pen, and selling his sketches for what he could get, buying now a brush and then some paints with the scanty proceeds, and working upon his bits of canvas with all the ardor of a Raphael himself.

A man sat before an easel in a crowded studio one day, give the last touch to a painting that stood before him. It pictured the figure of a lad, ragged and forlorn, lying asleep beneath some sheltering trees. At first that seems all there was to be seen upon the canvas; but if one looked closer one was able to discover another figure amid the vaporous, soft glooms of the place. It grew ever more distinct, until one had no difficulty in distinguishing the form of a maiden, fair and frail as a dream. She was bending over the slumbering body of the boy, as if to arouse him to life by the whispered words she was breathing against his cheek.

The artist scrawled his signature in the corner of his completed work and set the canvas in its frame, and then stood before it, scrutinizing it closely.

"'The Waking Soul!' - I wonder if that is a good name for it?" murmured he to himself. And then, after a moment, he said to the pictured lad, -

"Well, Larry, little fellow, the dream's come true; and here we are, you and I, - you, Larry, and I, Lawrence, - with the 'wish grown strong to an endeavor, and the endeavor to an achievement.' Are you glad, Boy?"

BETTY'S BY-AND-BY

"'One, two, three!
The humble-bee!
The rooster crows,
And away she goes!'"

And down from the low railing of the piazza jumped Betty into the soft heap of new-mown grass that seemed to have been especially placed where it could tempt her and make her forget - or, at least, "not remember" - that she was wanted indoors to help amuse the baby for an hour.

It was a hot summer day, and Betty had been running and jumping and skipping and prancing all the morning, so she was now rather tired; and after she had jumped from the piazza-rail into the heap of grass she did not hop up nimbly at once, but lay quite still, burying her face in the sweet-smelling hay and fragrant clover, feeling very comfortable and contented.

"Betty! Betty!"

"Oh dear!" thought the little maid, diving still deeper into the light grass, "there's Olga calling me to take care of Roger while she gets his bread and milk ready. I don't see why she can't wait a minute till I rest. It's too hot now. Baby can do without his dinner for a

Julie M. Lippmann

minute, I should think, - just a minute or so. He won't mind. He 's glad to wait if only you give him Mamma's chain and don't take away her watch. Ye-es, Olga, - I 'll come - by and by."

A big velvety humble-bee came, boom! against Betty's head, and got tangled in her hair. He shook himself free and went reeling on his way in quite a drunken fashion, thinking probably that was a very disagreeable variety of dandelion he had stumbled across, - quite too large and fluffy for comfort, though it was such a pretty yellow.

Betty lazily raised her head and peered after him. "I wonder where you're going," she said, half aloud.

The humble-bee veered about and came bouncing back in her direction again, and when he reached the little grass-heap in which she lay, stopped so suddenly that he went careering over in the most ridiculous fashion possible, and Betty laughed aloud. But to her amazement the humble-bee righted himself in no time at all, and then remarked in quite a dignified manner and with some asperity, -

"If I were a little girl with gilt hair and were n't doing what I ought, and if I had wondered where a body was going and the body had come back expressly to tell me, I think I 'd have the politeness not to laugh if the body happened to lose his balance and fall, - especially when the body was going to get up in less time than it would take me to wink, - I being only a little girl, and he being a most respected member of the Busy-bee Society. However, I suppose one must make allowances for the way in which children are brought up nowadays. When I was a little -"

"Now, *please* don't say, 'When I was a little girl,' - for you never were a little girl, you know," interrupted Betty, not intending to be saucy, but feeling rather provoked that a mere humble-bee should undertake to rebuke her. "Mamma always says, 'When I was a little girl,' and so does Aunt Louie, and so does everybody; and I 'm tired of hearing about it, so there!"

The humble-bee gave his gorgeous waistcoat a pull which settled it more smoothly over his stout person, and remarked shortly, -

"In the first place, I was n't going to say, 'When I was a little girl.' I was going to say, 'When I was a little *leaner*,' but you snapped me up so. However, it's true, isn't it? Everybody was a little girl once, were n't she? - was n't they? - hem! - confusing weather for talking, very! And what is true one ought to be glad to hear, eh?"

"But it is n't true that everybody was once a little girl; some were little boys. There!"

"Do you know," whispered the humble-bee, in a very impressive undertone, as if it were a secret that he did not wish any one else to hear, "that you are a very re-mark-a-ble young person to have been able to remind me, at a moment's notice, that some were little boys? Why-ee!"

Betty was a trifle uncomfortable. She had a vague idea the humble-bee was making sport of her. The next moment she was sure of it; for he burst into a deep laugh, and shook so from side to side that she thought he would surely topple off the wisp of hay on which he was sitting.

Julie M. Lippmann

"I think you 're real mean," said Betty, as he slowly recovered himself; "I don't like folks to laugh at me, now!"

"I 'm not laughing at you *now*," explained the humble-bee, gravely; "I was laughing at you *then*. Do you object to that?"

Betty disdained to reply, and began to pull a dry clover-blossom to pieces.

"Tut, tut, child! Don't be so touchy! A body can laugh, can't he, and no harm done? You 'd better be good-tempered and jolly, and then I 'll tell you where I 'm going, - which, I believe, was what you wished to know in the first place, was n't it?"

Betty nodded her head, but did not speak.

"Oho!" said the humble-bee, rising and preparing to take his departure. And now Betty discovered, on seeing him more closely, that he was not a humble-bee at all, but just a very corpulent old gentleman dressed in quite an antique fashion, with black knee-breeches, black silk stockings, black patent-leather pumps with large buckles, a most elaborate black velvet waistcoat with yellow and orange stripes across, and a coat of black velvet to correspond with the breeches; while in his hand he carried a very elegant three-cornered hat, which, out of respect to her, he had removed from his head at the first moment of their meeting. "So we are sulky?" he went on. "Dear, dear! That is a very disagreeable condition to allow one's self to relapse into. H'm, h'm! very unpleasant, very! Under the circumstances I think I 'd better be going; for if you 'll believe me, I 'm pressed for time, and have none to waste, and only came back to converse with you because you addressed a civil question to me, which, being a gentleman, I was bound to answer. Good -"

He would have said "by;" but Betty sprang to her feet and cried: "Please don't leave me. I 'll be good and pleasant, only please don't go. *Please* tell me where you 're going, and if - if you would be so good, I 'd like ever and ever so much to go along. Don't - do - may I?"

The little gentleman looked her over from head to foot, and then replied in a hesitating sort of way: "You may not be aware of it, but you are extremely incautious. What would you do if I were to whisk you off and never bring you back, eh?"

"You don't look like a kidnapper, sir," said Betty, respectfully.

"A what?" inquired the little gentleman.

"A kidnapper," repeated Betty.

"What's that?" questioned her companion.

"Oh, a person who steals little children. Don't you know?"

"But why *kidnapper*?" insisted the little old man.

"I suppose because he naps kids. My uncle Will calls Roger and me 'kids.' It is n't very nice of him, is it?" she asked, glad to air her grievance.

"Child-stealer would be more to the point, I think, or

infant-abductor," remarked the old gentleman, who saw, perhaps, how anxious Betty was for sympathy, and was determined not to give her another opportunity of considering herself injured.

He seemed to be very busy considering the subject for a second or so, and then he said suddenly: "But if you want to go, why, come along, for I must be off. But don't make a practice of it, mind, when you get back."

"You have n't told me where yet," suggested Betty.

"True; so I have n't," said the old gentleman, setting his three-cornered hat firmly on his head and settling the fine laces at his wrists. "It's to By-and-by. And now, if you 're ready, off we go!"

He took Betty's hand, and she suddenly found herself moving through the air in a most remarkable manner, - not touching the ground with her feet, but seeming to skim along quite easily and with no effort at all.

"If you please, Mr. -" She paused because she suddenly remembered that she did not know the name of the gentleman who was conducting her on so delightful a journey.

"Bombus," said he, cheerfully, - "B. Bombus, Esq., of Clovertop Manse, Honeywell."

"But you 're not a minister, are you?" inquired Betty.

"No; why?" returned the gentleman, quickly.

"Because you said 'Manse.' A manse is a minister's house, is n't it?" asked Betty.

"No, not always," Bombus replied. "But I call my place Clovertop Manse because it belongs to me and not to my wife, do you see? I call it Manse because it *is* a man's. It is perfectly plain. If it was a woman's, I 'd say so."

"Well, I don't think you 're much of a *humble*-bee -" began Betty, and then caught herself up short and stopped.

Mr. Bombus gave her a severe look from under his three-cornered hat, but did not reply at once, and they advanced on their way for some little time in silence. Then the gentleman said:

"I 've been thinking of what you said about my not being a humble-bee. Of course I am not a humble-bee, but you seemed to lay considerable stress on the first part of the word, as if you had a special meaning. Explain!"

Poor Betty blushed very red with shame and confusion; but the gentleman had a commanding way with him and she dared not disobey.

"I only meant, sir," she stammered, - "I only meant - I - did n't think you were very humble, because you seemed very proud about the place being yours. I thought you were 'stuck up,' as my brother says."

"Stuck up? Where?" queried Mr. Bombus, anxiously. "Pray don't make such unpleasant insinuations. They quite set my heart to throbbing. I knew - I mean I saw a humble-bee once," he remarked impressively, "and would you believe it, a little boy caught him and impaled him on a pin. It was horrible. He died in the most dreadful agony, - the bee, not the boy, - and then the boy secured him to the wall; made him fast there. So he was stuck up. You surely can't mean -"

"Oh, no, indeed! I meant only proud," replied Betty, contritely; for Mr. Bombus's face had really grown pale with horror at the remembrance of the bee's awful fate, and she was very sorry she had occasioned him such discomfort.

"Then why did n't you say only 'proud'?" asked her companion, sharply. "You said 'proud,' and then added 'stuck up.'"

Betty thought it was about time to change the subject, so she observed quietly that By-and-by seemed a long way off.

"Of course it is a long way off," replied her companion. "Don't you wish it to be a long way off?"

Betty hesitated. "Well, I don't think I ever wished much about it. Can you tell me how many miles it is from some place I know about? You see, Mr. Bombus, I am pretty sure it is n't in the geography. At least, I don't remember that I ever saw it on the map. Could n't you tell me where it is?"

Mr. Bombus considered a moment, And then asked, "Do you know where Now is?"

Betty thought a minute, and then replied, "I suppose it is Here, sir."

"Right!" assented the old gentleman, promptly. "Now, if you had said There, it would have been wrong; for

Then is There. You see, this is the way: When we have lived in Now until it is all used up, it changes into Then, and, instead of being Here, is There. I hope it's plain to you. Well, you asked me where By-and-by was. That 's the very thing about it: it never was, not even *is*; it's always *going to be*, and it's generally a rather long way from Now; so, if you know where Now is, you can make your own calculations as to the distance of By-and-by."

"But I don't know anything about calculating distances," said Betty, dolefully.

"It does n't matter," remarked Mr. Bombus; "for even if you did you could n't apply it in this case. But we 're getting on in our journey. Yes, indeed, we seem to be really getting on."

"Why, I should hope so!" returned Betty. "It seems to me I never flew so fast in all my life before and for such a long time. If we were n't getting on, I think I should be discouraged. We seem to be almost running a race, we go so quickly."

"We are running a race," observed Mr. Bombus.

Betty opened her eyes wide and said: "Why, *I* did n't know it. When did we begin?"

"When we started, Child. Pray, don't be stupid!" replied her friend, a little severely.

"But with whom are we running it?" queried Betty.

"With Time," whispered Mr. Bombus, confidentially. "One always has to beat him before one can get to

By-and-by. And then it depends on one's self whether one likes it or not after one gets there."

But even as he spoke Betty seemed to feel herself hurried along more rapidly than ever, as if she were making a final effort to outstrip some one; and then she was brought to so sudden a standstill that she had to do her best to keep from falling forward, and was still quite dizzy with her effort when she heard a panting voice say, "That last rush quite took away my breath!" and found herself being addressed by Mr. Bombus, who was very red in the face and gasping rather painfully, and whom she had, for the moment, forgotten.

Betty said: "My, Mr. Bombus, how warm you are! Sit right down on the grass and cool off before we go any farther, please."

"Oh, dear, no!" objected her companion. "That would be terribly imprudent, with these cold autumn winds blowing so; and winter just over there. I 'd catch my death, Child."

"Why, I 'm sure," replied Betty, "I don't know what you mean. It's as summer as it can be. It's a hot August day, and if you can't sit outdoors in August, I 'd like to know when you can."

"Allow me to inform you, my dear child, that it isn't August at all; and if you had half an eye you 'd see it, let alone feel it. Do these leaves look as if it were August?" and he pointed to a clump of trees whose foliage shone red and yellow in the sunlight.

Betty started. "Good gracious!" she exclaimed. "How

came they to change so early?"

"It *isn't* early," explained Mr. Bombus. "It's the last of October, - even later, - and keeps getting more so every minute."

"But," insisted Betty, "it was August when I first saw you, a few hours ago, and -"

"Yes, *then* it was August," assented Mr. Bombus; "but we 've got beyond that. We 're in By-and-by. Did n't you hear your mother say it would be October by and by, and it *is* October. Time is jogging on, back there in the world; but we beat him, you see, and are safe and sound - far ahead of him - in By-and-by. Things are being done here that are always *going* to be done behind there. It's great fun."

But at these words Betty's face grew very grave, and a sudden thought struck her that was anything but "great fun." Would she be set to doing all the things she had promised to do "by and by"?

"I 'm afraid so," said Mr. Bombus, replying to her question though she had only *thought* it. "I told you it depended on one's self if one were going to like By-and-by or not. Evidently you 're *not*. Oh! going so soon? You must have been a lazy little girl to be set about settling your account as quick as this. See you later! Good -"

But again he was not permitted to say "by," for before he could fairly get the word out, Betty was whisked away, and Mr. Bombus stood solitary and alone under a bare maple-tree, chuckling to himself in an amused fashion and, it must be confessed, in a spiteful.

Julie M. Lippmann

"It 'll be a good lesson for her. She deserves it," he said to himself; and Betty seemed to hear him, though she was by this time far away.

Poor child! she did not know where she was going nor what would take place next, and was pretty well frightened at feeling herself powerless to do anything against the unknown force that was driving her on.

But even while she was wondering she ceased to wonder; and what was going to happen had happened, and she found herself standing in an enormous hall that was filled with countless children, of all ages and nationalities, - and some who were not children at all, - every one of whom was hurrying to and fro and in and out, while all the time a voice from somewhere was calling out names and dates in such rapid succession that Betty was fairly deafened with the sound. There was a continual stir in the assembly, and people were appearing and reappearing constantly in the most perplexing manner, so that it made one quite dizzy to look on. But Betty was not permitted to look long, for in the midst of the haranguing of the dreadful voice she seemed to distinguish something that sounded strangely familiar.

"Betty Bleecker," it called, "began her account here when she was five years old by the World calculation. Therefore she has the undone duties of seven years - World count - to perform. Let her set about paying off her debt at once, and stop only when the account is squared;" whereupon Betty was again whisked off, and had not even time to guess where, before she found herself in a place that reminded her strangely of home and yet was not home at all. Then a wearisome round of tasks began.

She picked up pins, she opened doors, she shut windows, she raised shades, she closed shutters, she ran errands, she delivered messages, she practised scales, she studied lessons, she set her doll-house in order and replaced her toys, she washed her face and brushed her hair, she picked currants and stoned raisins, she hung up her skipping-rope and fastened her sash; and so she went on from one thing to another until she was almost ready to cry with weariness and fatigue. Half the things she did she had forgotten she had ever promised to do. But she had sent them into By-and-by, and here they were to be done, and do them she must. On and on she went, until after a while the tasks she had to perform began to gain a more familiar look, and she recognized them as being unkept promises of quite a recent date. She dusted her room, she darned her stockings, she mended her apron, she fed her bird, she wrote a letter, she read her Bible; and at last, after an endless space and when tears of real anguish were coursing down her cheeks, she found herself amusing the baby, and discovered that she had come to the last of her long line of duties and was cancelling her debt to By-and-by.

As soon as all was finished she felt herself being hurried, still sobbing and crying, back to the place from which she had started, and on entering heard the same voice she had listened to before, say, -

"Betty Bleecker's account is squared. Let a receipted bill be given her; advise her to run up no more accounts, and send her home."

At these words Betty wept afresh, but not now from sorrow, but from gladness at the thought of returning home. And before she could even realize it, she was standing beside Mr. Bombus again, with something in her hand which she clutched tightly and which proved to be a signed receipt for her debt to By-and-by. Then she heard her companion say, -

"Like to look about a bit before you leave? By-and-by's a busy place; don't you think so?"

And Betty replied promptly, "Oh, no, sir - yes, sir - not at all, sir - if you please, sir;" quite too frantic at the thought of having to go back, even for a moment, to answer the questions.

But all the while she was very angry with Mr. Bombus for bringing her there, quite forgetting she had pleaded with him to do so; and his smiling at her in that very superior fashion provoked her sadly, and she began upbraiding him, between her sobs and tears, for his unkindness and severity.

"It would only have been harder in the end," replied her companion, calmly. "Now you 've paid them and can take care not to run up any more debts; for, mark my words, you 'll have to square your account every time, and the longer it runs the worse it will be. Nothing in the world, in the way of responsibility, ever goes scot-free. You have to pay in one way or another for everything you do or leave undone, and the sooner you know it the better."

Betty was sobbing harder than ever, and when she thought she caught a triumphant gleam in Mr. Bombus's eyes and heard him humming in an aggravating undertone, "In the Sweet By-and-by," she could restrain herself no longer, but raised her hand and struck him a sounding blow. Instantly she was most deeply repentant, and would have begged his pardon; but as she turned to address him, his cocked hat flew off, his legs doubled up under him, his eyes rolled madly, and then with a fierce glare at her he roared in a voice of thunder: "BET-TY!"

And there she was in the soft grass-heap, sobbing with fright and clutching tightly in her hand a fistful of straw; while yonder in the wistaria-vine a humble-bee was settling, and a voice from the house was heard calling her name:

"Betty! BET-TY!"

Julie M. Lippmann

THE WHITE ANGEL

Once upon a time there lived in a far country a man and his wife, and they were very poor. Every morning the man went his way into the forest, and there he chopped wood until the sky in the west flushed crimson because of the joy it felt at having the great sun pass that way; and when the last rim of the red ball disappeared behind the line of the hills, the man would shoulder his ax and trudge wearily home.

In the mean time the wife went about in the little hut, making it clean and neat, and perhaps singing as she worked, - for she was a cheery soul. Well, one day - perhaps it was because she was very tired and worn; I do not know - but one day she sat down by the door of her hut, and was just about to begin sewing on some rough piece of hempen cloth she had in her lap, when, lo! she fell asleep.

Now, this was very strange indeed, and even in her dream she seemed to wonder at herself and say: "I have never slept in the daytime before. What can it mean? What will Hans think of me if he should come home and find me napping in the doorway and his supper not ready for him, nor the table spread?"

But by and by she ceased to wonder at all, and just sat leaning against the door-frame, breathing softly, like a little child that is dreaming sweet dreams.

But presently the trees of the forest began to bow their heads, and the wind chanted low and sweet, as though in praise; the sun shot a golden beam along the foot-path, and made it glitter and shine, and then a wonderful silence seemed to fall on the place, and before her stood an angel, white-robed and beautiful. He said no word, but stretched out his arms to her and would have taken her to his heart, but that she cried out with a great fear, -

"Ah, no! not yet; I cannot go yet. I am young, and life is sweet. I cannot give it up. Do not take me yet!" and she fell at his feet.

The angel smiled sadly and said: "Be it so, then. I will not take, I will give. But bemoan thou not thy choice when the life thou deemest so sweet seems but bitter, and thy load more heavy than thou canst bear. I will come once again;" and smiling down upon her, he was gone.

With a great cry she rose; for the light that shone all about the angel seemed to make many things clear to her, and she would have been glad to do his will, but it was now too late.

The tree-tops were motionless again, the wind had ceased its chanting, the sun had withdrawn its wondrous light, and along the worn little foot-path came Hans with his ax upon his shoulder. She said nothing to him about her dream, for she was afraid; but she got his supper for him, and when the stars had slipped out from behind the spare clouds, he had dropped to sleep and left her to lie awake gazing at

Julie M. Lippmann

them silently until each one seemed to smile at her with the smile of an angel, and then it was morning, and she had slept, after all, and the sun was shining.

After that Christina was always busy preparing for the gift the angel had promised her, and she sang gayly from morning till night, and was very glad.

So the months rolled along, and the memory of her dream had almost faded from Christina's mind. Then one day a strange sound was heard in the little hut, - the sound of a baby's crying. Hans heard it as he came along, and it made his eyes shine with gladness. He hastened his steps, and smiled to himself as he thought of his joy in having a little child to fondle and caress.

But at the door he paused, for he heard another sound besides that of the baby's voice. It was Christina's, and she was weeping bitterly.

In a moment he was beside her, and then he knew. There he lay, - their little son. The angel's gift, - a wee cripple. Not a bone in all his little body was straight and firm. Only his eyes were strangely beautiful, and now they were filled with tears.

"It were better he had died, and thou, also, Christina," sobbed Hans. "It were better we had all three died before this sorrow was brought upon us." But Christina only wept.

So the years went by, and the baby lived and grew. It was always in pain, but it seldom cried; and Christina could not be impatient when she saw how uncomplaining the little child was.

When he was old enough she told him what she never told any one before, - the story of the angel; and his eyes were more beautiful than ever when she wept because she could not suffer it all alone, but must see him suffer too. And while Hans scarcely noticed the boy, Christina spent all her time thinking of him and teaching him, and together they prayed to the white angel to bless them.

But as the years went on many men came to the forest and felled the trees, not with axes but with huge saws; and so Hans was turned away, for no one wanted a wood-chopper now. And so they were in great trouble; and Hans grew rough and ill-tempered, and did not try to use the saw, nor would he ask the men to let him work. He would only stand idly by, and often Christina thought the blessings she prayed for were turned to curses; but she never told the child her sorrow, and still they prayed on to the white angel to bless them. When Christina saw Hans would really do no work, she said no more, but sewed and spun for the men about who had no wives, and in this way she earned enough to buy food and wood. It was very little she could earn, and she often grew impatient at the sight of Hans smoking idly in the doorway; but when she said a hasty word the boy's eyes seemed to grow big with a deep trouble, and she would check herself and work on in silence. But the more she worked, the idler grew Hans and the more ill-tempered; and he would laugh when he heard them pray to the angel to bless them. Instead of blessings new sorrow seemed to be born every day; for Hans was injured by a falling tree, and was brought home with both his legs crushed, and laid helpless and moaning on the rough bed.

These were weary days for Christina; but she did not

rebel, even when Hans swore at her and the child, and made the place hideous with his oaths.

"You brought us all these troubles, you wretched boy!" he would say. "Don't talk to *me* of patience. Why don't you pray to your angel for curses, and then we may have some good luck again? As it is, you might as well pray to the Devil himself."

But the child only drew Christina's head closer to his poor little misshapen breast, and whispered to her, "It is not so, is it, little mother?"

And she always answered: "No, dear heart. They are indeed blessings if we will only recognize them. It we prayed only for happiness, we might think the white angel heard us not; but we pray for blessings, and so he sends us what we pray for, and what he sends is best."

Then again the boy's eyes shone with a great light, and there seemed a radiance about his head; but Christina was kissing his shapeless little hands and did not see.

One day Christina was returning with a fresh bundle of work in her arms, when, just as she came in sight of the hut, she saw a pillar of smoke rise black and awful to the sky from the rude roof of the place.

In a moment she felt a horrible fear for Hans and the child. Neither of them could move; and must they lie helpless and forsaken in the face of such a fearful death? She ran as though her feet were winged. Nearer and nearer she came, and now she saw the flames rise and lick the smoky column with great lapping tongues of fire.

Nearer and nearer she came, and the crowd of men about the hut stood stricken and dared not venture in.

"It is of no use," they screamed. "We did not know soon enough, and now it is too late; we should smother if we tried to save them."

But she tore her way through the crowd and flung herself into the burning place.

Hans, writhing and screaming, had managed to drag himself near the door; and thinking, "The child is more fit for heaven, I will save Hans first," she lifted him in her arms and carried him outside. It was as though some great strength had been given her, for she carried him as if he had been a little child. Then into the hut she went once more, and to the bed of the child. But now the flames were licking her feet, and the smoke blinded her. She groped her way to the bed and felt for the boy, but he was not in his accustomed place; and she was about to fling herself upon the little couch in despair, when a great light filled the place, - not the red light of the flames, but a clear white flood such as she had only seen once before.

There stood the white angel, radiant, glorious; and looking up she saw him smiling down at her with the eyes of the boy.

"I am come again," he said. "When you would not give me your life, I gave you mine, and it was spent in pain and torture. Now that you would gladly give yours to spare me, you are to taste the sweetest of all blessings. The lesson is over; it is done." And he took her in his arms and she was filled with a great joy, for she knew the angel had answered all her prayers. She remembered the words: "He that findeth his life shall lose it; and he that loseth his life for my sake shall find it."

The men outside waited in vain for Christina, and when she did not come they shook their heads and some of them wept. They did not know.

IN THE PIED PIPER'S MOUNTAIN.

It was a great honor, let me tell you; and Doris, as she sat by the window studying, could not help thinking of it and feeling just a wee bit important.

"It is n't as if I were the oldest girl," said she to herself. "No, indeed; I 'm younger than most of them, and yet when it came to choosing who should speak, and we were each given a chance to vote, I had the most ballots. Miss Smith told me I could recite anything I chose, but to be sure it was 'good,' and that it was not 'beyond me.' Well, this is n't 'beyond me.' I guess;" and she began: -

> "Hamelin Town 's in Brunswick,
> By famous Hanover City;
> The river Weser, deep and wide,
> Washes its walls on the southern side, -
> A pleasanter spot you never spied.
> But, when begins my ditty,
> Almost five hundred years ago,
> To see the townfolk suffer so
> With vermin was a pity."

For she had chosen Browning's "Pied Piper of Hamelin." That was surely "good;" and if it was long, why, it was "so interesting." As she went along she could almost see the rats as they "fought the dogs and killed the cats." She could almost see the great Mayor tremble as the people flocked to him and threatened to "send him packing" if he did n't find some means to rid them of those awful rats. She could almost hear the Pied Piper's voice as he offered to clear the town of the pests; and it seemed to her she could hear the music of his pipe as he stepped into the street and began to play, while the rats from every hole and cranny followed him to the very banks of the Weser, where they were drowned in the rolling tide.

It seemed awful that after promising the Piper those fifty thousand guilders, the Mayor should break his word; and it certainly was terrible, when the Piper found he had been duped, that he should again begin to pipe, and that the children - yes, every one in Hamelin Town - should follow him just as the rats had done, and that by and by he should lead them to the mountain-side, that it should open, and that, lo! after they had all passed in, it should close again, leaving only one little lame boy outside, weeping bitterly because he had not been able to walk fast enough to keep up with the merry crowd. It was all so distinct and plain.

She wondered where the children went after the hillside shut them in. She wondered what they saw. She thought the Piper's music must have been very odd indeed to charm them so. She could almost hear - *What was that*? She gave a start; for sure as you live, she heard the sound of a fife piping shrill and loud round the corner. She flung down the book and ran into the street. The air was cold and sharp and made her shiver, but she did not stop to think of that; she was listening to that Piper who was coming around the side of the house, - nearer and nearer. She meant to follow him, whoever he was. There! How the wind whistled and the leaves scurried!

Wind! Leaves! Why, it was the Pied Piper himself with his puffed cheeks and tattered coat; and before him ran the host of children, dancing, as they went, to the tune of the Piper's fife.

Away - away -

With a bound Doris left the door-step and followed after, running and fluttering, skipping and skurrying, sometimes like a little girl and sometimes like a big leaf, - she had n't time to ask herself which she really was; for all the while she was listening to that wonderful fife as it whistled and wailed, shrieked and sighed, and seemed to coax them on all the while.

She followed blindly after the rest of the whirling crowd.

Away they went, always more and more, - away they went, clear out of town and into the bare country, - away they went; and the Piper behind them made his fife-notes shriller and louder, so that all could hear, and they seemed to be carried along in spite of themselves.

It was like a race in a dream. Their feet seemed not to touch the ground. The leaves rustled - no, the children chattered as they fluttered - no, hurried along. Doris could catch little sentences here and there; but they seemed to be in a strange tongue, and she did not understand. But by and by she grew very familiar with the sounds, and, strangely enough, she found she could make out the meaning of the queer words.

Julie M. Lippmann

"It 's German," she thought; "I know they're talking German;" and so she listened very attentively.

"Sie ist eine Fremde," she heard one say to another; "sie gehoert nicht zu uns," - which she immediately knew meant: "She is a stranger; she doesn't belong to us."

"Nein," replied the other; "aber sie scheint gut und brav zu sein." At which Doris smiled; she liked to be thought "good and sweet."

On and on they went; and after a time things began to have a very foreign look, and this startled Doris considerably.

"We can't have crossed the ocean," she thought. But when she asked her nearest neighbor where they were and whether they had crossed the Atlantic, he smiled and said, -

"Ja, gewiss; wir sind in Deutschland. Wir gehen, schon, nach Hamelin," - which rather puzzled Doris; for she found they had crossed the sea and were in Germany and going to Hamelin.

"It must be the Piper's wonderful way," she thought.

But she did not feel at all homesick nor tired nor afraid; for the Piper's fife seemed to keep them all in excellent spirits, and she found herself wondering what she would do when they came to the fabled hill-side, - for she never doubted they would go there. On they went, faster and faster, the Piper behind them playing all the while.

She saw the broad river; and all the children shouted, "Die Weser."

One little flaxen-haired girl told her they were nearing Hamelin.

"It used to have a big wall around it, with twenty towers and a large fort; but that was all blown up by the French, years and years ago," she explained.

"But it has a chain-bridge," she remarked proudly, - "a chain-bridge that stretches quite across the Weser."

Doris was just about to say: "Why, that's nothing! We have a huge suspension bridge in New York;" but the words seemed to twist themselves into a different form, and the memory of home to melt away, and she found herself murmuring, "Ach, so?" quite like the rest of the little Teutons.

But at length the fife ceased playing, and the children stopped.

There they were in quaint old Hamelin, with its odd wooden houses, and its old Munster that was all falling to ruin, and its rosy-cheeked children, who did not seem to notice the new-comers at all.

"We must be invisible," thought Doris; and indeed they were.

Then the Pied Piper came forward and beckoned them on, and softly they followed him to the very hill-side, that opened, as Doris knew it would, and they found themselves in a vast hall. A low rumbling startled Doris for a moment, but then she knew it was only the

Julie M. Lippmann

hill-side closing upon them. She seemed to hear a faint cry as the last sound died, away, and was tempted to run back, for she feared some child had been hurt; but her companion said, -

"It can't be helped, dear; he *always* gets left outside, and then he weeps. You see he is lame, and he cannot keep up with us."

So Doris knew it was the self-same little lad of whom Browning had written in his story of the Piper.

What a chattering there was, to be sure; and what a crowd was gathered about the Piper at the farther end of the hall! Every once in a while all the children would laugh so loudly that the very ceiling shook. It was such a merry throng.

"Tell me," said Doris to her little neighbor, - "tell me, are you always so gay here? Do you never quarrel? and have you really lived in this hillside all this long, long time, - ever since the Piper first came to Hamelin five hundred years ago?"

"Ja, wohl," replied the girl, nodding her flaxen head. "We are always so happy; we never quarrel; therefore we are ever young, and what thou callest five hundred years are as nothing to us. Ah! we are well cared for here, and the Piper teaches us, and we him; and we play and frolic and sometimes travel, 'und so geht's.'"

"But what can you teach *him*?" asked Doris, wondering.

"Ah! many things. We teach him to tune his fife to the sounds of our laughter, so that when he travels he may pipe new songs. Ah! Thou foolish one, thou thoughtest him the *wind*. And we teach him to be as a little child, and then he keeps young always, and his heart is warm and glad. And we teach him - But thou shalt see;" and she nodded again, and smiled into Doris's wondering eyes.

The hall they were in was long and wide, and hung all about the walls were the most beautiful pictures, that seemed to shift and change every moment into something more strange and lovely. And as Doris looked she seemed to know what the pictures were, - and they were only reflections of the children's pure souls that shone out of their eyes.

"How beautiful!" she thought.

But the Piper was singing to them now; and as she drew nearer him she saw he had two little tots in his arms, and was putting them to sleep on his breast.

So the children were still while the Piper sang his lullaby, and presently the two little ones began to nod; and the Piper did not move, but held them to his kind heart until they were fast asleep. Then he rose and carried them away and laid them down somewhere. Doris could not see where, but it must have been far enough away to be out of the sound of their voices; for when he came back he did not lower his tones, but spoke up quite naturally and laughed gayly as he said, -

"Well, what now, Children? Shall we show the new friend our manufactory?"

And they were all so anxious to do whatever he proposed that in a moment they had formed quite a bodyguard about the Pied Piper, and were following and leading him down the vast hall.

"What is the manufactory?" asked Doris of a boy who happened to be beside her.

"Wait and thou shalt see!" he replied. "We always are patient until the Herr Piper is ready to tell us what he wishes; then we listen and attend."

Doris would have felt that the boy was snubbing her if his eyes had not been so kind and his voice so sweet. As it was she took it all pleasantly, and determined to ask no more questions, but to content herself with as much information as the Piper was willing to bestow upon her.

But now they had passed out of the first great hall and into another that seemed even more vast. At first it seemed quite empty to Doris, but as soon as her eyes grew accustomed to the strange light, she saw its walls were flanked by any number of wee spinning-wheels; and above them on shelves lay stacks of something that looked like golden flax, and shimmered and glittered in a wonderful way. The floor was carpeted with something very soft and of a tender, fresh green, and Doris's feet seemed to sink into it at every step; and then a sweet perfume seemed to rise up like that one smells on an early spring-day when one goes into the country and is the first to lay foot on the fresh young grass. The ceiling was so high that at first Doris thought it was no ceiling at all, but just the sky itself, and it was a deep, clear blue.

"This is our Spring-room, little Doris," explained the Piper. "Now, Children!"

And at these words they broke away from him, leaving only Doris by his side; and each group began a different task. One new to the stacks of gold and separated them into long, heavy skeins; while another spun the threads back and forth till they sparkled and danced and seemed to turn into sunbeams that at length broke away and glanced into the blue above, where they played about just as the sunlight does on a bright spring-day. Others, again, knelt down upon the soft carpet, and seemed to be whispering something very sweet to some one or something hidden below; and before very long up sprang long, tender shoots, and then thin buds appeared, and by and by the buds swelled and burst, and then where every bud had been was a flower. And all this time there had been a sound as of falling drops that seemed to be keeping time to a soft little melody the children were crooning.

The Piper, looking at Doris's wondering face, said, smiling: "Thou dost not comprehend, dear heart? Well, I will explain. As I said, this is our Spring-room, and in it all the sunshine and flowers and clouds and rain are made that go to make up a spring day. They," he said, pointing to the first group, "are separating the golden skeins so that they can be spun into sunbeams. It takes great patience before they are completely finished; and if one of the spinners should sigh while weaving, it would ruin the beam and make it dull and heavy. So, you see, the sunbeam-children must be very light-hearted. Then those others are coaxing the flowers to spring up and bud. After they are all well above ground the flower-children hide a secret in the heart of each blossom, and a very beautiful secret it is, and so wonderful that very few ever succeed in finding it out. But it is worth searching for, and one or two world-people have really discovered it. Thou mayst guess what a difficult task is that of my flower-children; for at first the flowers are drowsy and would prefer to slumber yet awhile; and my children must whisper to them such beautiful thoughts that they forget everything else and spring up to hear more. The singing thou nearest is the lullaby the rain-children are singing to the drops. Thou knowest that the clouds are the rain-cradles, and when my children sing slumber songs and rock the clouds gently to and fro, the drops grow sleepy and forget to fall. But sometimes they are too restless to remain in their beds, and then they fall to earth; and if we could wait so long we might hear the children teach them their patter-song. But we have much else to see, and must go forward. Now, Children!"

At this there was a slight commotion while the deft hands put aside their tasks; but it was over in a moment, and the Piper once more in the midst of the merry crowd, who laughed gayly and chattered like magpies, while Doris looked her admiration and delight, and the Piper smiled approvingly.

"The next is the Summer-room," he said, as they wandered on. "Thou seest we are never idle. The world is so large, there is always plenty to do; and what would become of it if it were not for the children? They are the ones who make the world bright, little Doris; and so everything depends upon their keeping their hearts glad; and one 's heart cannot be glad if one's soul is not beautiful. Thou thoughtest not so much depended upon the children, didst thou, dear heart?"

Oh, the wonders of that Summer-room! The perfect chorus that rose as the fresh young voices taught the birds to sing; the beauty of the rainbows, the glory of the sunsets. It was all so wonderful that Doris scarcely knew how to show her appreciation of it all.

The Autumn-room was scarcely less bewildering, and the Winter-room was so dazzling that Doris shut up her eyes for very wonder.

In the Autumn-room all the little musicians set about transposing the melody of the bird-songs from the major to the minor key, and they taught the Piper to bring his fifing into harmony with their voices. The small artists began changing the sky-coloring, and brought about such wonderful effects that it was marvellous to see, and Doris could scarcely realize at all that such wonders could be.

After they had shown her the Winter-room and had seen her amazement at the glory of the snow-crystals and the mysterious way in which the rainbow colors were hidden in the ice, the Piper nodded his head, and they all turned back and began to retrace their steps.

"I suppose thou didst wonder where we had been when thou didst join us, little friend," said the Piper. "I will tell thee. In the spring we all set out on our travels; for my children must see and learn, besides showing and teaching others. So in the spring we leave this place and go into the world. Then I go wandering about with my fife north and south, east and west, and the people think me the wind. But my dear children could not bear such fatigue; so they take up their abode in the trees, and remain there guiding the seasons and seeing that all is well; whispering to me as I pass and to one another, and singing softly to the stars and the clouds, and then every one mistakes and thinks them simply rustling leaves. Then, when I have finished my journeying, I give them a sign, and they dress themselves in gala-costume, - for joy at the thought of coming home, - and when every one is gay in red, purple, and yellow, they all slip down from the trees and away we go. People have great theories about the changing of the foliage, but it is a simple matter; as I tell you, it is only that my children are getting ready to go home.

"During the winter we leave the world to sleep, for it grows very weary and needs rest. My children arrange its snow-coverlets for it, and then it slumbers, and the moon and stars keep watch. So now thou knowest all, little maid, and thou canst be one of us, and make the world bright and glorious if thou wilt. It only needs a beautiful soul, dear Doris; then one remains ever young, and can work many wonders."

"Oh, I will, I will!" cried Doris, instantly.

"But," said the Piper, "it takes such long experience. Thou seest my children had long years of it; and until thou canst make life bright within, thou couldst not venture without. But if thou wilt try, and be content to work in patience, - there are many children who are doing this -"

"Oh, I will, I will!" said Doris, again.

Then the children laughed more happily than ever, and the Piper raised his fife to his lips and blew a loud, glad note.

What was this? The children had disappeared, the Piper was gone, and Doris sat by the window, and her book had dropped to the floor. She rubbed her eyes.

"It was a dream," she said. "It is the Piper's wonderful way; he has left me here to work and wait, so that I may make the world beautiful at last." And she smiled and clapped her hands as the wind swept round the corner.

MARJORIE'S MIRACLE

"Shall we have to wait until all these folks have been taken?" asked Marjorie, looking from the crowd of people who thronged the fashionable photograph-gallery to her mother, who was threading her way slowly through the press to the cashier's desk.

"Yes, dear, I 'm afraid so. But we must be patient and not fret, else we shall not get a pleasant picture; and that would never do."

While she paid the clerk for the photographs and made her arrangements with him as to the desired size and style, Marjorie busied herself with looking around and scanning the different faces she saw.

"There!" she thought; "what for, do you s'pose, have I got to wait for that baby to have its picture taken? Nothing but an ugly mite of a thing, anyway! I should n't guess it was more than a day old, from the way it wiggles its eyes about. I wonder if its mother thinks it's a nice baby? Anyhow, I should think I might have my picture taken first. And that hump-backed boy! Guess I have a right to go in before him! He 's not pretty one bit. What a lovely frock that young lady has on, - all fluffy and white, with lace and things! She keeps looking in the glass all the time, so I guess she knows she 's pretty. When I am a young lady I 'll be prettier than she is, though, for my hair is goldener than hers, and my eyes are brown, and hers are nothing, but plain blue. I heard a gentleman say the other day I had 'a rare style of beauty,' he did n't know I heard (he was talking to Mamma, and he thought I had gone away, but I had n't). I 'm glad I have 'a rare style of beauty,' and I 'm glad my father 's rich, so I can have lovely clothes and - Seems to me any one ought to see that I 'm prettier than that old lady over there; she 's all bent over and wrinkled, and when she talks her voice is all kind of trembly, and her eyes are as dim - But she 'll go in before me just the same, and I 'll get tireder and tireder, until I - Mamma, won't you come over to that sofa, and put your arm around me so I can rest? I 'm as sleepy as I can be; and by the time all these folks get done being *taken*, I 'll be dead, I s'pose. *Do* come!"

Her mother permitted herself to be led to the opposite side of the room, where a large lounge stood, and seating herself upon it, took her little daughter within the circle of her arm; whereupon Marjorie commenced complaining of the injustice of these "homely" people being given the advantage over her pretty self.

"Oh, Marjorie, Marjorie!" whispered her mother, "what a very foolish little girl you are! I think it would take a miracle to make you see aright. Don't you know that that dear baby is very, very sick, and that probably its sad little mother has brought it here to have its picture taken, so that if it should be called away from her, she might have something to gaze at that looked like her precious little one? And that poor crippled boy! He has a lovely face, with its large, patient eyes and sensitive mouth. How much better he is to look at than that young woman you admire so much, whose beauty does not come from her soul at all, and will disappear as soon as her rosy cheeks fade and her hair grows gray! Now, that sweet old lady over there is just a picture of goodness; and her dear old eyes have a look of love in them that is more beautiful than any shimmer or shine you could show me in those of your friend Miss Peacock."

"Why do you call her 'Miss Peacock'? You don't know her, do you?" queried Marjorie.

"No, I don't know her in one sense, but in another I do. She is vain and proud, and the reason I called her Miss Peacock was because of the way in which she struts back and forth before that pier-glass, - just like the silly bird itself. But I should not have called her names. It was not a kind thing to do, even though she *is* so foolish; and I beg her pardon and yours, little daughter."

Marjorie did not ask why her mother apologized to her. She had a dim sort of an idea that it was because she had set her an example that she would be sorry to have her follow. Instead, she inquired suddenly, -

"How do they take pictures, Mamma? I mean, what does the man do, when he goes behind that queer machine thing and sticks his head under the cloth, and then after a while claps in something that looks like my tracing-slate and then pops it out again? What makes the picture?"

"The sun makes the picture. It is so strong and clear that though it is such a long distance away it shines down upon the object that is to be photographed and reflects its image through a lens in the camera upon a plate which is *sensitized* (that is, coated with a sort of gelatine that is so sensitive that it holds the impression cast upon it until by the aid of certain acids and processes it can be made permanent, that is, lasting). I am afraid I have not succeeded in explaining so you understand very clearly; have I, Sweetheart?"

Marjorie nodded her head. "Ye-es," she replied listlessly. "I guess I know now. You said - the sun - did - it; the sun took our pictures. It's very strange - to think - the sun - does - it."

"Come, Marjorie! Want to go travelling?" asked a voice.

"No, thank you; not just now," replied Marjorie, slowly. "I am going to have my photograph taken in a little while, - just as soon as all these stupid folks get theirs done. I should n't have time to go anywhere hardly; and besides it 'd tire me, and I want to look all fresh and neat, so the picture will be pretty."

"But suppose we promised, honor bright -"

"Begging your pardon," broke in another voice, "that's understood in any case, - a foregone conclusion, you know. Our honor would *have* to be bright."

"Suppose we promised faithfully," continued the first voice, pretending not to notice the interruption, "to bring you back in time to go in when your turn comes, would n't you rather take a journey with us and see any number of wonderful things than just to sit here leaning against your mother's arm and watching these people that you think so 'stupid'?"

"Of course," assented Marjorie, at once. "It 's awful

tiresome, - this; it makes me feel just as sleepy as can be. But what 's the use of talking? I can't leave here or I 'd lose my chance, and besides Mamma never lets me go out with strangers."

"We 're not strangers," asserted the voice, calmly; "we are as familiar to you as your shadow, - in fact, more so, come to think of it. You have always known us, and so has your mother. She 'd trust you to us, never fear! Will you come?"

Marjorie considered a moment, and then said: "Well, if you're perfectly sure you 'll take care of me, and that you 'll bring me back in time, I guess I will."

No sooner had she spoken than she felt herself raised from her place and borne away out of the crowded room in which she was, - out, out into the world, as free as the air itself, and being carried along as though she were a piece of light thistle-down on the back of a summer breeze.

That she was travelling very fast, she could see by the way in which she out-stripped the clouds hurrying noiselessly across the sky. One thing she knew, - whatever progress she was making was due, not to herself (for she was making absolutely no effort at all, seeming to be merely reclining at ease), but was the result of some other exertion than her own. She was not frightened in the least, but, as she grew accustomed to the peculiar mode of locomotion, became more and more curious to discover the source of it.

She looked about her, but nothing was visible save the azure sky above her and the green earth beneath. She seemed to be quite alone. The sense of her solitude began to fill her with a deep awe, and she grew strangely uneasy: as she thought of herself, a frail little girl, amid the vastness of the big world.

How weak and helpless she was, - scarcely more important than one of the wild-flowers she had used to tread on when she was n't being hurried through space by the means of - she knew not what. To be sure, she was pretty; but then they had been pretty too, and she had stepped on them, and they had died, and she had gone away and no one had ever known.

"Oh, dear!" she thought, "it would be the easiest thing in the world for me to be killed (even if I *am* pretty), and no one would know it at all. I wonder what is going to happen? I wish I had n't come."

"Don't be afraid!" said the familiar voice, suddenly. "We promised to take care of you. We are truth itself. Don't be afraid!"

"But I *am* afraid," insisted Marjorie, in a petulant way, "and I 'm getting afraider every minute. I don't know where I 'm going, nor how I 'm being taken there, and I don't like it one bit. Who are you, anyway?"

For a moment she received no reply; but then the voice said: "Hush! don't speak so irreverently. You are talking to the emissaries of a great sovereign, - his Majesty the Sun."

"Is *he* carrying me along?" inquired Marjorie presently, with deep respect.

"Oh, dear, no," responded the voice; "we are doing that. We are his vassals, - you call us beams. He never condescends to leave his place, - he could not; if he were to desert his throne for the smallest fraction of a second, one could not imagine the amount of disaster that would ensue. But we do his bidding, and hasten north and south and east and west, just as he commands. It is a very magnificent thing to be a king -"

"Of course," interrupted Marjorie; "one can wear such elegant clothes, that shine and sparkle like everything with gold and jewels, and have lots of servants and -"

"No, no," corrected the beam, warmly. "Where did you get such a wrong idea of things? That is not at all where the splendor of being a king exists. It does not lie in the mere fact of one 's being born to a title and able to command. That would be very little if that were all. It is not in the gold and jewels and precious stuffs that go to adorn a king that his grandeur lies, but in the things which these things represent. We give a king the rarest and the most costly, because it is fitting that the king should have the best, - that he is worthy of the best; that only the best will serve one who is so great and glorious. They mean nothing in themselves; they only describe his greatness. The things that one sees are not of importance; it is the things that they are put there to represent. Do you understand? I don't believe you do. I 'll try to make it more clear to you, like a true sunbeam. Look at one of your earth-kings, for instance. He is nothing but a man just like the rest of you; but what makes him great is that he is supposed to have more truth, more wisdom, more justice and power. If he has not these things, then he would better never have been a king; for that only places him where every one can see how unworthy he is, - makes his lacks only more conspicuous. Your word *king* comes from another word, *koenning*; which comes from still another word, *canning*, that means *ableman*. If he is not really an ableman, it were better he had never worn ermine. And there, too; ermine is only a fur, you know. It is nothing in itself but fur; but you have come to think of it as an emblem of royalty because kings use it. So you see, Marjorie, a thing is not of any worth really except as it represents something that is great and noble, something *true*."

Marjorie was very silent for a little; she was trying to understand what the sunbeam meant, and found it rather difficult. After a while she gave it up and said, -

"Will you tell me how you are carrying me, and where we are going, and all about it?"

"Certainly," replied the beam, brightly. "You are in a sort of hammock made out of threads of sunshine. We sunbeams can weave one in less than no time, and it is no trouble at all to swing a little mortal like you way out into the clearness and the light, so that a bit of it can make its way into your dark little soul, and make you not quite so blind as you were."

"Why, I 'm not blind at all," said Marjorie, with a surprised pout. "I can see as well as anything. Did you think I couldn't?"

"I *know* you can't," replied the beam, calmly. "That is, you can't see any farther than the outside part of things, and that is almost worse than seeing none of them at all. But here we are nearing the court of the king. Now don't expect to see *him*, for that is impossible. He is altogether too radiant for you; your eyes could not bear so much glory. It would be just as if you took one of your own little moles or bats (creatures that are used to the dark) and put them in the full glare of a noonday sun. The sun would be there, but they could not see it, because their eyes would be too weak and dim. Even yourself, - have n't you often tried to look the sun full in the face? Yes; and you have had to give it up and turn your face away because it hurt your eyes. Well, his Majesty only lets the world have a glimpse of his glory. But here we are at our journey's end."

With these words Marjorie felt herself brought to a gentle halt, and found herself in a place most wondrously clear and light and high, from which she could look off, - far, far across and over and down to where something that looked like a dim ball was whirling rapidly.

"That is your earth," whispered the sunbeam in her ear, - "the earth that you have just left."

Marjorie was so astounded that for a time she was unable to say a word. Then she managed to falter out: "But it always looked so big and bright, and now it is nothing but a horrid dark speck -"

"That is just it, Marjorie, - just what I said. When you look at the world simply as a planet, it is small and dark enough, not nearly so large as some of the others you see about you; but when you look at it as a place on which God has put his people to be good and noble, to work out a beautiful purpose, then - But wait a moment."

Marjorie felt a strange thrill pass through her; across her eyes swept something that felt like a caressing hand, and when she looked again everything was changed, and she seemed gazing at a wonderful sort of panorama that shifted and changed every moment, showing more lovely impressions each instant.

"What is it?" she gasped, scarcely able to speak for delight and breathless with amazement.

"Only pictures of your world as it really is. Pictures taken by his Highness the Sun, who does not stop at the mere outer form of things, but reveals the true inwardness of them, - what they are actually. He does not stop with the likeness of the surface of things; he makes portraits of their hearts as well, and he always gets exact likenesses, - he never fails."

Marjorie felt a sudden fear steal over her at these words; she did not precisely know why, but she had a dim sort of feeling that if the sun took photographs of more than the outside of things (of the hearts as well), some of the pictures he got might not be so pretty, perhaps. But she said nothing, and watched the scroll as it unrolled before her with a great thrill of wonderment.

With her new vision the world was more beautiful than anything she had ever imagined. She could see everything upon its surface, even to the tiniest flower; but nothing was as it had seemed to her when she had been one of its inhabitants herself. Each blade of grass, each tree and rock and brook, was something more than a mere blade or tree or rock or brook, - something so much more strange and beautiful that it almost made her tremble with ecstasy to see.

"Now you can see," said the voice; "before you were blind. Now you understand what I meant when I said the objects one sees are of themselves nothing; it is what they represent that is grand and glorious and beautiful. A flower is lovely, but it is not half so lovely as the thing it suggests - but I can't expect you to understand *that*. Even when you were blind you used to love the ocean. Now that you can see, do you know why? It is because it is an emblem of God's love, deep and mighty and strong and beautiful beyond words. And so with the mountains, and so with the smallest weed that grows. But we must look at other things before you go back -"

"Oh, dear!" faltered Marjorie, "when I go back shall I be blind again? How does one see clear when one goes back?"

"Through truth," answered the beam, briefly.

But just then Marjorie found herself looking at some new sights. "What are these?" she whispered tremblingly.

"The *proofs* of some pictures you will remember to have half seen," replied the beam.

And sure enough! with a start of amaze and wonder she saw before her eyes the people who had sat in the crowded gallery with her before she had left it to journey here with her sunbeam guide; but, oh! with such a difference.

The baby she had thought so ugly was in reality a white-winged angel, mild-eyed and pitying; while the hump-backed boy represented a patience so tender that it beautified everything upon which it shone. She thought she recognized in one of the pictures a frock of filmy lace that she remembered to have seen before;

but the form it encased was strange to her, so ill-shapen and unlovely it looked; while the face was so repulsive that she shrank from it with horror.

"Is that what I thought was the pretty girl?" she murmured tremulously.

"Yes," replied the beam, simply.

The next portrait was that of the silver-haired old lady whom Marjorie had thought so crooked and bowed. She saw now why her shoulders were bent. It was because of the mass of memories she carried, - memories gathered through a long and useful life. Her silver hair made a halo about her head.

"The next is yours," breathed the voice at her side, softly. "Will you look?"

Marjorie gave a quick start, and her voice quivered sadly as she cried, -

"Oh, blessed sunbeam, don't force me to see it! Let me go back and try to be better before I see my likeness. I am afraid now. The outside prettiness is n't anything, unless one's spirit is lovely too; and I - I could not look, for I know - I know how hateful mine would be. I have learned about it now, and it's like a book; if the story the book tells is not beautiful, the pictures won't be good to see. I have learned about it now, and I know better than I did. May I - oh, may I try again?"

She waited in an agony of suspense for the answer; and when it came, and the voice said gently, "It is your turn next," she cried aloud, -

"Not yet, oh, not yet! Let me wait. Let me try again."

And there she was, with her cheeks all flushed and tear-stained, her hair in loose, damp curls about her temples, and her frock all rumpled and crushed in her mother's arms; and her mother was saying, -

"Bad dreams, sweetheart? You have had a fine, long nap; but it is your turn next, and I have had to wake you. Come, dear! Now we must see if we cannot get a good likeness of you, - just as you really are."

WHAT HAPPENED TO LIONEL

It is not to be supposed that such things happen every day. If they were to happen every day, one would get so familiar with them that they would not seem at all extraordinary; and if there were no extraordinary things in the world, how very dull one would be, to be sure! As it is - But to go back.

The beggar had stood before the area-gate for a long time, and no one had paid the slightest attention to him. He was an old man with long gray hair, and a faded, ragged coat, whose tatters fluttered madly to and fro every time the wind blew. He was very tall and gaunt, and his back was bent. On his head was a big slouched hat, whose brim fell forward over his eyes and almost hid them entirely in its shadow. He carried a basket upon one arm, and a cane with a crook for a handle hung upon the other. He seemed very patient, for he was waiting, unmurmuringly, for some one to come in answer to the ring he had given the area-bell some fifteen minutes before. No one came, and he appeared to be considering whether to ring again or go away, when Lionel skipped nimbly from his chair by the drawing-room window, slipped noiselessly down the basement stairs, and opened the area-door just in time to prevent the beggar from taking his departure.

"What do you want, sir?" inquired Lionel, politely,

Julie M. Lippmann

through the tall iron gate.

The beggar turned around at the sound of the child's voice, and replied:

"I have come to beg -"

"Oh, yes, I know," cried Lionel, hurriedly (he was afraid some one might come, and then he would be snatched unceremoniously away from the open door, and the beggar sent smartly about his business by one of the pert-tongued maids); "but is it for cold victuals or money?"

The beggar looked down at the little lad, and a smile, half of pity, half of amusement, lit up his grave features for a moment. "I have come to beg," he said slowly, "that you will receive from me, not that you will give to me."

Lionel's eyes widened with amazement. "That I will receive from you?" he repeated slowly. "Then you are n't a beggar at all?"

"Most assuredly I am," responded the old man, promptly. "Do I not beg of you? What is a beggar? 'One who begs or entreats earnestly or with humility; a petitioner.' That is how your dictionary has it. It does n't say for what he begs or entreats. Where I come from things are so different, - there it is a mark of distinction, I can assure you, to be a beggar. One must have lived such a long life of poverty and self-sacrifice before one is permitted to beg - to beg others to receive one's benefits. Ah, yes, there it is so different!"

"Yes, it must be," assented Lionel. "Here beggars are

just persons who go about and ask for cold bits or pennies; and we don't think much of them at all."

"That is because they are not the right kind of almsfolk, nor you the right kind of almoners," responded the beggar; and then he repeated: "Ah, yes, there it is so different!"

"Where?" inquired Lionel. "Won't you tell me about it?"

"Dear child," replied the beggar, gently, "it can't be described. It must be seen to be appreciated. If you once entered into that estate, you would never wish to return to this."

"Is it as nice as all that?" questioned Lionel, eagerly. "Guess I 'll go, then. Will you take me ?" he asked.

The beggar smiled down at him kindly. "I can't take you, dear boy," he said. "I have to travel on. But I can set you on the road, and you will reach there in safety if you follow my directions."

Lionel waited breathlessly for the beggar to continue; but the man almost seemed to have forgotten his existence, for he was gazing dreamily over his head into the darkness of the hallway, apparently seeing nothing but what was in his own mind's eye.

"Well?" asked Lionel, a little impatiently. "You were going to give me the directions, you know."

"Oh, yes!" returned the beggar, with a slight start. "Well, the directions are: *Always turn to the right!*"

Lionel considered a moment, and then he said: "But if I always turn to the right I should n't get anywhere at all. I 'd be only going round and round."

"No, no!" replied the beggar, hastily; "you must always go *square*, you know. And you 'll find you 'll get along beautifully if you always keep to the right."

"But s'pose," suggested Lionel, "I come to a place where the road is to the left, - some of the roads might be not to the right, - some might go quite the other way."

"Yes," assented the beggar, wistfully. "They *all* go the other way, - that is, they *seem* to go the other way. But when they seem to go to the wrong and you don't see any that go to the right, just keep as near to the right as you can, and by and by you 'll see one and it will be lovely. But if you turn down to the wrong, you run a chance of losing your way entirely. It is always so much harder to go back."

"But are those all the directions you are going to give me?" inquired Lionel, with a doubtful glance.

"They are sufficient," replied the beggar. "You 'll find them sufficient;" and before Lionel could say another word the beggar had vanished from before his very eyes. He had not slipped away, nor slunk away, nor walked away, nor sped away, - he had simply vanished; and Lionel was left alone behind the grated door of the area-way gazing out upon a vacant space of pavement where, an instant before, the beggar had stood. The little boy rubbed his eyes and looked again. No, the beggar was gone, in very truth, and had left not so much as a rag behind him. But, look! what was that?

Something lay upon the stone step just outside the gate, and it gleamed brightly from out its dusky corner. Lionel reached up and unlatched the heavy fastening. The great gate swung slowly in, and Lionel stepped briskly out. He bent down and grasped the shining object; it proved to be a little rule, and it was made of solid gold. He clasped it to his bosom.

"How beautiful!" he murmured. "Now I can measure things and carve them with my jack-knife, and they 'll be just exactly right. Before they have n't been quite straight, and when I 'd try to put the parts together they wouldn't fit; but now -"

And then suddenly the thought flashed across his mind: "Perhaps it belongs to the beggar and he might want it;" and without a moment's thought to his bare head, he passed quickly through the gateway and out into the street.

"It's such a beautiful rule," he thought, as he flew along. "I never saw such a darling. If it were mine, how I should hate to lose it! I must certainly find him and give it back to him; for I know he must feel just as I should if it were mine."

It never entered into his head to keep the thing; his one idea seemed to be to find the beggar and return to him his property. But before very long his breath began to come in gasps, and he found himself panting painfully and unable to run any farther. He paused and leaned against the huge newel-post at the foot of some one's outer steps. His cheeks were aglow, his eyes flashing, his thick curls rough and tumbled, and his bang in fine disorder. The deep embroidered cuffs and collar upon his blouse were crushed and rumpled; his little Zouave

Julie M. Lippmann

jacket was wind-blown and dusty, and his pumps splashed with mud from the gutter-puddles through which he had run. At home they would have said he "looked like distress;" but here, leaning wearily against the post, he was a most picturesque little figure.

Suddenly he felt a light touch upon his head, and then his bang was brushed back from his temples as though by the stroke of some kindly hand. He looked up, and there beside him stood the oddest-looking figure he had ever seen.

The stranger was clad from head to foot in a suit of silver gray. Upon his head he wore a peaked cap, upon his feet were the longest and most pointed of buskins; his doublet and hose were silver gray, and over his shoulders hung a mantle about which was a jagged border made after the most fantastic design, which shone and glittered like ice in sunlight. About his hips was a narrow girdle from which hung a sheathed dagger whose hilt was richly studded with clear, white crystals that looked to Lionel like the purest of diamonds.

Lionel felt that when he spoke it would probably be after some old-century fashion which he could scarcely understand; but there he was mistaken, for when the stranger addressed him, it was in the most modern manner and with great kindliness.

"Well, my son," he said cheerily, "tired out? I saw you run. You have a fine pair of heels. They have good speed in them."

"I wanted to catch up with someone, - an old beggar-man who lost something in our area-way. I wanted to return it to him," explained Lionel, breathlessly.

The stranger gazed down at him more kindly than ever. "So? But one can't expect to catch up with folks when one gets *winded* and has to stop every now and then for breath. Better try my mode."

"Please, sir, what is your mode?" inquired Lionel, with his politest manner.

"To begin with," explained his companion, "I have to accomplish the most astonishing feats in the manner of speed. Literally I have to travel so fast that I am in two places at once. You will the better believe me when I tell you who I am, - Jack Frost, at your service, sir. Now, by what means do you think I manage it ?"

"I 'm sure I don't know. I should like immensely to find out," Lionel returned.

"How do you get to places yourself?" inquired Jack Frost. "Do you always run?"

"Oh, no, indeed. I almost always ride on my bicycle. Then I can *go* like anything, 'specially down *coasts*. Upgrades are kind of hard sometimes, but not so very. Oh, I can go quick enough when I have my bicycle."

"Now then," broke in Jack Frost, "you use a bicycle, - that is, a machine having two wheels. Now *I* use a something having but one wheel; consequently it goes twice as fast, - oh! much more than twice as fast."

"One wheel?" repeated Lionel, thoughtfully; "seems to me I never heard of that kind of an one."

"Suppose you guess," proposed Jack Frost. "I 'll put it in the form of a conundrum: If a thing having two wheels is called a *bi*cycle, what would a thing having but one be called?"

"Oh, that's an old one. I 've heard that before, and the answer is, a wheelbarrow, you know."

Jack Frost shook his head, "I see I shall have to tell you," he said. "If a thing having two wheels is called a *bi*cycle, a thing having but one would naturally be an *i* cicle. Of course you might have known I should use an icicle."

"But oh, Mr. Frost," objected Lionel, "I never saw an icicle with a wheel in my life, and I never saw one go either."

"That's because you have n't seen me on one; and even if you had seen me on one, you wouldn't have known it, - we travel so fast. Did you ever notice that when things are going at the very rapidest rate possible, they seem to be standing perfectly still? That's the way with icicles. They have tremendous speed in them. They go so fast you can't realize it, and then when they are slowing up they don't do it with a clumsy jerk as bicycles do; they just gradually melt out of sight."

"Yes, I 've seen them do that. I 've seen them go that way," admitted Lionel. "But will you take me to the beggar? I'm 'fraid I sha'n't be able to give him his rule if I don't hurry up."

"But do you know in what direction he went?" asked Jack Frost. "If one wants to catch up with any one, one needs to have *some* idea of the direction he took. It's quite a *desideratum,* - when you get home, look that up."

Then Lionel felt deeply mortified. "What a silly I was!" he said. "Perhaps I was going just the opposite way from the one he went. Oh, dear! how can I ever give him back his rule? It is such a beauty. If it had been mine, I 'd just hate to lose it."

"Let us examine it," suggested Jack Frost, "and see if there is any sign upon it that would help to discover its owner;" and without a moment's doubt or hesitation Lionel drew it from his pocket and held it up for Jack Frost to see.

Then for a little space they both gazed at it carefully; Jack Frost bending down his tall head to get a nearer view of it, and Lionel standing upon the tips of his toes to accomplish the same purpose.

"Oh, see, see!" cried the boy, joyously. "It says, 'LIONEL, - HIS RULE FOR LIFE.' That means I can keep it for always, does n't it? Forever 'n' ever."

"It means," explained Jack Frosty gravely, "that you can keep it, - yes. But it means you are to measure your life with it. You are always to use it in everything you do. Then you 'll be *true*, and whatever you do will be *straight* and *square*."

"Why, that's what he said himself. He said I must always 'go square.' That was when he was giving me directions how to reach the beautiful place he came from. He called it an estate; and he said if I ever got there I 'd never want to come away. As long as I 'm on the way I guess I 'll try to find that place. Will you take me?"

"I 'm afraid," replied Jack Frost, with a very kindly seriousness, - "I 'm afraid one must depend on one's self in order to reach that place. But I 'll tell you what I will do; I 'll stay with you for a bit, and, perhaps, having company will hearten you, so if you happen to come across any specially bad places just at first, you won't be discouraged. And I want to tell you that if you are ever in doubt as to the way and no one is there to give you advice, just set yourself to work and use your rule and you 'll come out right. Now don't forget!" and with these words he vanished.

"Why, I thought he was going to stay with me," murmured Lionel, despondently. "He was so jolly, and I liked him so much. He said he wouldn't leave me just yet -"

"Nor have I," rejoined the hearty voice close by his ear. "But I can't neglect my business, you know; and at this moment I 'm here and 'way off in Alaska too. Stiff work, is n't it?"

But in spite of this Lionel heard him whistling cheerily beside him.

The boy trudged on, and every once in a while he and his invisible comrade would converse together in the most friendly manner possible, and Lionel did indeed feel encouraged by the knowledge of Jack Frost's companionship. But by and by, after quite a long time, Lionel noticed that when he addressed his unseen fellow-traveller the voice that came to him in reply seemed rather far away and distant, and later became lost to him altogether.

Then he knew that Jack Frost had left him for a season, and he felt quite lonely and deserted and was about to drop a tear or two of regret, when all at once, at his very feet, opened a new way which he had not noticed before. It looked bright and inviting, and wound along in the most picturesque fashion, instead of lying straight and level before him, as did the road from which it branched.

He was just about to turn down this fascinating side-path, and was in the very act of complaining about his loneliness and bemoaning it aloud, when he happened to notice that the sky looked a little overcast; the air had grown heavy and still, and a strange, sad hush brooded over everything; while the bare branches upon the trees appeared to droop, and the one or two birds that had perched upon them uttered low, plaintive little sounds that were disheartening to hear.

Lionel was struck with so great an awe that he entirely forgot himself and his sorrow; and in that one moment the skies seemed to brighten, the air to lighten, and the trees and birds had grown songful again.

"What does it mean?" he asked himself anxiously; and then, all at once, he bethought himself of Jack Frost's advice in case he ever was in doubt as to the course he was to take, and in a twinkling had whipped out his rule and was down on his knees applying it in good earnest. Then how glad he was that he had not turned into the inviting by-path, for his little rule showed how crooked and wrong it was, - whole yards and yards away from the right; and he knew he must have met with some mishap, or at the very least have wasted any amount of precious time trying to retrace his steps and regain the place upon which he now stood.

He was so relieved to think he had been saved from making such a sad mistake that he began to whistle merrily, and in an instant the whole world about him was bright of hue and joyous again, and looking, he saw, to his amazement, that the bare branches were abud.

"It's spring," he cried happily, and leaped along his way toward the right. In a flash the tempting little by-path had curled up like a scroll and disappeared from view; and then Lionel knew that it had not been real at all, but only imaginary, and he was more grateful than ever that he had not followed its lead.

"Now, you good little rule," said he, addressing the shining object in his hand, "I 'll put you in my breast-pocket and keep you safe and warm next to my heart. Then you 'll be ready if I want you again." And he was just about to thrust it in his bosom, when his eyes were caught by something unusual upon its surface, and on examining it very closely he saw, in exquisitely chased characters, the words, -

> Nor sigh nor weep o'er thine own ills;
> Such plaining earth with mourning fills.
> Forget thyself, and thou shalt see
> Thyself remembered blessedly.

For some time after he had read the lines he was plunged in thought. They seemed to teach him a lesson that it took him some little time to learn.

"I don't know why it should make the world sad if one complains," he mused. "But I s'pose it does. I s'pose one has n't any right to make things unpleasant for other people by crying about things. One ought to be brave and not bother folks with one's troubles. Well, I 'll try not to do so any more, because if it's going to make things so unpleasant it can't be right."

And this last word seemed to link in his mind his escape from the complaint of his loneliness and the by-path down which he did not turn; and he was so long trying to unravel the mystery of the connection that before he knew it he had almost stumbled into quite a bog, and there, in front of him, sat a wee child, - just where two roads met, - and he had well-nigh run over her in his carelessness.

"Oh, bother!" said he, - for he was irritated at the thought of having only so narrowly escaped doing himself serious damage, - "what do you get in a fellow's way for? You - " But the poor little mite gazed up at him so sadly, and wept so piteously at his hasty words that he paused suddenly and did not go on.

He looked down the two paths. The one was wide and curving, the other narrow and straight; the one was bordered with rich foliage, the other was bare and sandy. He might have run lightly along the one, he would have to toil wearisomely along the other. What wonder that his foot was turning in the direction of the first! But a queer pricking in his bosom and the child's cry stopped him.

He slowly drew forth his rule and began to measure, while the little one sobbed, -

"I 'm so told I tan't walt any more. My foots are all tired out, and I want sumpin to eat;" and there he found himself just on the verge of making a fearful blunder. He got up from his knees and turning to the tiny maid, said kindly, -

"There, there! don't cry, dear! We 'll fix you all right;" and he stripped off his jacket and wrapped it about her, taking her in his arms, and trudging on with his burden along the more difficult way. But it was the right one, and he knew it; and so his heart was light, and he did not have time to think of his own weariness; for all the time he was trying to comfort his forlorn little companion. And so well he succeeded that in no time at all she was asleep on his shoulder. Then he sat down by the roadside, and holding her still in his arms, began to think.

"There I was a little while ago complaining - no, not quite complaining, but *almost* - because I hadn't anybody to keep me company. Now I 've got some-body with a vengeance. She's awful heavy. But, oh, dear! What a narrow escape I had! I might have run into that bog, and that would have been a 'pretty how d 'ye do,' as Sarah says. I was so busy thinking I forgot everything, and ran almost over little Sissy; and that shows, I s'pose, how without meaning it one can hurt somebody if one does n't look out."

And then, very carefully, so as not to wake his sleeping charge, he slipped his hand into his pocket and drew out his rule again.

"What a good friend you are!" he said to it. "I really think you 're better than any sword or poniard a body could have. You 've saved me from danger twice now, and - " But here he stared at it in dumb surprise, for even as he looked he saw appear upon its polished surface the words, -

Deep is the bog in which they sink
Who ne'er on others' sorrow think;
Deeper the joy in which they rest
Who 've served the weary and distressed.

And, sure enough, he felt so happy he could have sung aloud in spite of his weariness and fatigue.

But I could not begin to tell you of all his experiences, nor how unfailingly his little rule helped him to meet them successfully.

He thought a great deal about it and its magical power; but once or twice he did get to wondering why it should point to the straight path when the winding one was so much the prettier to see.

"Are the right ways always the ones we should n't take if we had our own way?" he thought. "Why is it that the right one always seems not so pretty as the other? Seems to me some one told me once that the curved lines were 'the lines of beauty.'" But before he had time fairly to consider the subject, his rule, which he happened to be holding in his hand, showed him this little verse, -

"Straight is the line of duty,
Curved is the line of beauty;
Follow th' one and thou shalt see
The other ever following thee."

And this was always the way. Whenever Lionel was puzzled about anything, his rule always made it clear to him. And by and by, after he had met with all sorts of adventures, he began to wonder whether he was ever going to see the beggar again or reach his wonderful estate.

It was on a very beautiful day that he wondered this, and he was more than a little happy because he had just been applying his rule to unusually good effect, when, lo! there beside him stood the subject of his thoughts. But oh! how changed he was!

Every rag upon him glowed and shimmered with a wondrous lustre, and the staff he carried blazed with light, while the basket upon his arm overflowed with the most beautiful blessings.

"I thought," said the new-comer, "that I might risk giving you this encouragement. It will not make you content to go no farther on *now*. It will make you long to strive for greater good ahead. You will not reach it until you have travelled a lifetime; but you will not despair, for you are being so blessed. I have been permitted to give you a great gift. It is for that I was begging you that day. See, what a privilege it is to be able to beg so -"

"Oh, yes," cried Lionel; "you were going to beg me to accept the little rule, were n't you? And you left it for me when you disappeared, and it is a beauty, and it is gold, and it does strange, wonderful things for me, and - and -" In his enthusiasm he drew it from his breast and held it up, when, lo! it curved about his hand until it formed a perfect, beautiful circle. From its shining rim shot up points of radiance, and it was no more a simple little rule, but a golden crown fit for a king to wear.

Lionel gazed at it in mute wonderment, and the beggar put out his hand and touched it lovingly.

"When your journey is done you shall wear it, lad," he said; and then Lionel closed his eyes for very ecstasy, and then -

But when extraordinary things are just on the point of getting *too*extraordinary, they are sure to meet with some sort of an interruption, and after that they are quite ordinary and every-day again. So when Lionel opened his eyes there he was curled up in the chair by the drawing-room window, and it had grown very dark and must have been late, for one of the maids was tripping softly about the room, lighting the lamps and singing as she did it.

MARIE AND THE MEADOW-BROOK

A little maid sat sadly weeping while the sunbeams played merrily at hide-and-seek with the shadows that the great oak branches cast on the ground; while the warm summer wind sang softly to itself as it passed, and the blue sky had not even a white cloud with which to hide the sad sight from its eyes.

"Why do you weep?" asked the oak-tree; but Marie did not hear it, and her tears tell faster than ever.

"Why are you so sad?" questioned the sunbeams; and they came to her gently and tried to peep into her eyes.

But she only got up and sat farther away in the shadow, and they could do nothing to comfort her. So they danced awhile on the door-step; and then the sun called them away, for it was growing late.

And still the little maid sat weeping; and if she had not fallen asleep from very weariness, who knows what the sad consequences might not have been?

"How warm it is!" murmured the dandelions in the meadow. "Our heads are quite heavy, and our feet are hot. If it was not our duty to stand up, we would like nothing better than to sink down in the shade and go to sleep; but we must attend to our task and keep awake."

"What can you have, you wee things, to keep you busy?" asked the tall milkweed that grew near the fence-rails; and the mullein-stalk beside it echoed, -

"What, indeed?"

"Now, one can understand one so tall as I having to stand upright and do my duty; but you, - why, you are no taller than one of my green pods that I am filling with floss -"

"And not half so tall as one of my leaves that I must line with velvet," interrupted the mullein-stalk again.

The dandelions looked grieved for a moment, but answered brightly: "Why, don't you know? It must be because you live so far away - there by the fence - that you don't know we are here to pin the grass down until it grows old enough to know it must not wander off like the crickets, or to blow away like the floss in your own pods. Young grass is very foolish, - I think I heard the farmer call it green the other day, but we don't like the expression ourselves, - and it would be apt to do flighty things if we did n't pin it down where it belongs. When we have taught it its lesson, we can go to sleep. We always stay until the last minute, and then we slip on our white nightcaps, - so fluffy and light and soft they are, - and lo! some day we are gone, no one knows where but the wind; and he carries us off in his arms, for we are too tired to walk; and then we rest until the next year, when we are bright and early at our task again."

Then the milkweed and the mullein-stalk bowed very gravely and respectfully to the little dandelions, and said, -

Julie M. Lippmann

"Yes, we see. Even such wee things as you have your duties, and we are sorry you are so weary."

So the milkweed whispered to the breeze that the dandelions were too warm, and begged it to help them; but the breeze murmured very gently, -

"I don't know what is the matter with me, dear milkweed, but I am so faint, so faint, I think I shall die."

And sure enough, the next day the little breeze had died, and then they knew how they missed him, even though he had been so weak for the last few days; for the sun glared down fiercely, and the meadow thought it was angry, and was so frightened it grew feverish and parched with very dread.

"We wish our parasols were larger," sighed the toadstools; "but they are so small that, try as we may, we cannot get them to cast a large shadow, and now the breeze has died we have no messenger. If only one knew how to get word to the clouds!"

But the clouds had done such steady duty through the spring that they thought they were entitled to a holiday, and had gone to the mountain-tops, where they were resting calmly, feeling very grand among such an assembly of crowned heads.

Meanwhile the meadow grew browner and browner, and its pretty dress was being scorched so that by and by no one would have recognized it for the gay thing it had been a week ago. And still the sun glared angrily down, and the little breeze was dead.

Then the grasses laid down their tiny spears, and the dandelions bent their heads, and the locusts and the crickets and the grasshoppers called feebly, -

"Oh, little brook, cannot you get out of your bed and come this way?"

"Our hearts are broken," cried the daisies.

"We shall die," wailed the ragged-sailors. Then they all waited for the brook to reply; but she was silent, and call as they would they could get no answer.

"Hush!" whispered the springs. "Her bed is empty. Have n't you noticed how little she sang lately? The weeds must have fallen asleep and she has run away. You know they always hindered her."

They did not tell that they were too weak to feed the brook; so it had dried away. And still the sun glared down, and the little breeze was dead, and the brook had disappeared; while there on the door-step sat Marie weeping big tears, - for the little maid was always sad, and come when you would, there was Marie with her dark eyes filled and brimming over with the shining drops.

The beeches beckoned her from the garden; she saw them do it. Their long branches waved to her to come, like inviting arms; and still weeping, she stole quietly away.

"Come," whispered the gnarled apple-trees down in the orchard; and she threaded her way sadly among the trunks, while her tears fell splash, splash, on her white pinafore.

Julie M. Lippmann

"Here!" gasped the meadow-grass; and she followed on, sobbing softly to herself, as she sat down where, days ago, the brook had merrily sung.

"Why do you grieve?" asked the pebbles; and she heard them and answered, -

"Because I am so sad. Things are never as I want them, and so I cry. I am made to obey, and then, when the stars come out and I wish to stay up, I am sent to bed; and the next morning, when I am so sleepy I can hardly open my eyes, I am made to get up. Oh, this is a very sad world!" And she wept afresh.

Then the flowers and the grasses and the pebbles, seeing her tears, all said at once: "Would you like to stay here with us? Then you could stay awake all night and gaze at the stars, and in the morning you need not get up. You may lie in the brook's empty bed, and you need never obey your parents any more."

Marie was silent a moment, and then a hundred small voices said, "Do, oh, do!" And her tears fell faster and more fast, and larger and larger, for she felt more abused than ever now the meadow had shown her sympathy, as she thought. She kept dropping tears so quickly that by and by even her sobbing could scarcely be heard for the splash, splash, of the many drops that were falling on the white pebbles in the brook's bed.

How they fell! The brown eyes grew dim, and Marie could not see. She felt tiny hands pulling her down - down; and in a moment she had ceased to be a little girl and had become a brook, while her weeping was the murmur of little waves as they plashed against the stones.

Yes, it was true!

She need never go to sleep when the stars came out; she need never get out of her bed in the morning, - how could she when the strong weeds hindered her, - and how could a brook obey when people spoke?

And meanwhile the meadow grew gay again, for the brook cooled its fever; and by and by the dandelions tied on their large, fluffy nightcaps and disappeared, and the sun ceased to glare - for Marie was gone from the door-step with her weeping, and he need not look down on the ungrateful little maid who ought to have been so happy. The clouds came back; and when they heard how the meadow had suffered they wept for sympathy, and the underground springs grew strong, until one day there was a great commotion in the meadow.

A little bird had told the whole story of Marie's woe to the breeze, and he rose and sighed aloud; the trees tossed their arms about, because it was so wicked in a little girl to be ungrateful. The crickets said, "Tut, tut!" in a very snappy way; and at last the great wind rose, and whipped the poor brook until it grew quite white with foam and fear.

Then Marie knew how naughty she had been, and she made no complaint at her punishment. In fact, she bore it so meekly that after the wind had quieted down and the stormy flurry was over, she began to sing her quiet little song again, although she was very tired of it by this time, and was so meek and patient that all the meadow whispered:

"Good little thing now, - good little thing!" and then

Julie M. Lippmann

they told her how everything in the world, no matter how small it is, has a duty to perform, and should do its task cheerfully and gladly, and not weep and complain when it thinks matters are not going in the right way, but try to keep on with its task and relief will come.

Marie listened like an obedient little brook as she was, and was just going to float another merry little bubble to the little reeds below when she heard a voice say, "Give me my bed; I want it," and lo! There was the real brook come back. She pushed Marie aside and hurt her, though she seemed so gentle.

Marie tried to rise, but it was difficult; her limbs were stiff lying all this time in the meadow, her eyes were weary gazing at the sky, and her voice hoarse with the song she had been forced to sing.

She tried again, and this time she succeeded; and behold! there she was on the door-step, and the sun was going down.

NINA'S CHRISTMAS GIFTS

Hark! What was that?

Nina stood still in the wintry blast and listened. The wind rushed upon her wildly, and dragged her tattered skirt this way and that, and fleered at her, and whistled at her; and when she paid not the slightest attention to his cruel treatment of her, fled tumultuously down the street.

It was a wretched, shivering little figure that he left behind him, - a small girl, with coal-black hair escaping from the folds of a bright kerchief that was tied about it; with immense dark eyes, that seemed to light up her poor, pinched face and make it beautiful; with tattered dress and torn shoes, and with something clutched tightly beneath her arm, - something that she tried unsuccessfully to shield from the weather beneath her wretched rag of a shawl, that was so insufficient to shield even her. She was listening intently to the sounds of an organ that came pealing forth into the dusk from within the enormous church before whose doors she was standing.

Louder, fuller swelled the majestic cords, and then - Nina strained her ears to listen - and then the sweetest, tenderest voice imaginable seemed to be singing to her of all the most beautiful things of which she had ever dreamed. It drew her toward it by the influence of its plaintiveness; and first one step and then another she took in its direction until she was within the huge doors, and found herself standing upon a white marble floor, with wonderful paintings on the lofty ceiling above her head, and a sense of delicious warmth all about her. But, alas! where was the singer? The thrilling notes were still falling upon her ear with caressing sweetness; but they seemed to come from beyond, - from far beyond.

Before her she saw more doors. Perhaps if she slipped through these she might come in sight of the owner of the voice.

"It is the Santa Maria," murmured Nina to her heart. "And she is singing to the Bambinetto, - to the Santissimo Bambino. Ah, yes, it must be the Santa Maria, for who else could have a voice like that, - so sweet and soft, yet so heavenly clear and pure?"

No one she had ever heard could sing like that. Not Luisa who sang for pennies on the street, nor Guilia, nor Edwiga, nor yet Filomena herself, who was so proud of her voice and who carolled lustily all day long. No, no, it must be the Santa Maria.

Telemacho (Telemacho was a neighbor who played upon the harp and sometimes let Nina go with him on his tramps, to sing and play upon her fiddle, but oftener forced her to go alone, - they earned more so, he said) had often told her about the Santa Maria and the Gesu Bambino. Oh, it was a beautiful story, and - ah! ah! *of course* it was the Santa Maria. Was not this the Festa del Gesu Bambino? To be sure, it was, and she had forgotten. No wonder the Santa Maria was singing to the Bambinetto. To-morrow would be his birthday, his *festa*.

She would go to the blessed *Madre* and say, -

"Ah, *Madre mia*, I heard thee singing to the Bambino, and it was so sweet, *so* sweet, I could not help but follow, I *love* it so."

She stepped softly to the heavy doors, and with her whole weight bracing against one, pushed it softly open and passed through. Ah! But it was beautiful here.

Far, far above her head shone out dimly a hundred sparks of light like twinkling stars. And everywhere hung garlands of green, sweet-smelling garlands of green, that filled the place with their spicy fragrance. And no one need grow weary here for lack of resting-place. Why, it was quite filled with seats, soft-cushioned and comfortable. Nina stole into one of the pews and sat down. She was very tired, - very, very tired.

From her dim corner she peeped forth timidly, scarcely daring to raise her eyes lest the vision of the radiant Madonna should burst upon her view all too suddenly. But when at last she really gazed aloft to the point from which the tremulous voice sprung, no glorified figure met her view. She still heard the melting, thrilling tones, but, alas! The blessed singer - the Santa Maria - was invisible. All she could distinguish in the half-gloom of the place was the form of a man seated in the lofty gallery overhead. He was sitting before some kind of instrument, and his fingers slipping over the keys were bringing forth the most wonderful sounds. Ah, yes! Nina knew what music one could make with one's fingers. Did not Telemacho play upon the harp? Did not she herself accompany her own singing upon her fiddle, - her darling fiddle, which she clasped lovingly beneath her arm and bravely tried to shield from the weather? But surely, surely he could not be *playing* that voice! Oh, no! it was the Santa Maria, and she was up in heaven out of sight. It was only the sound of her singing that had come to earth. Poor little Nina! She was so often disappointed that it was not very hard to miss another joy. She must comfort herself by finding a reason for it. If there was a reason, it was not so hard. Nina had to think of a great many reasons. But nevertheless she could not control one little sigh of regret. She would so much have liked to see the Santa Maria. If she *had* seen her, she thought she would have asked her to give her a Christmas gift, - something she could always keep, something that no one could take from her and that would never spoil nor break. One had need of just such an indestructible possession if one lived in the "Italian Quarter." Things got sadly broken there. And - and - there were so few, so very few gifts. But it was warm and dim and sweet in here, - a right good place in which to rest when one was tired. She bent her head and leaned it against the wooden back of the seat, and her eyes wandered first to one interesting object and then to another, - to the tall windows, each of which was a most beautiful picture, and all made of wonderfully colored glass; to the frescoed walls garlanded with green and at last to the organ-loft itself, in which was the solitary figure of the musician, seated before that strange, many-keyed instrument of his, practising his Christmas music.

He had lit the gas-jets at either side of the key-board,

and they threw quite a light upon him as he played, and upon the huge organ-pipes above his head. Nina thought she had never seen anything as beautiful as were their illuminated surfaces. She did not know what they were, but that did not matter. She thought they looked very much like exceedingly pointed slippers set upright upon their toes. She fancied they were slippers belonging to the glorious angels who, Telemacho said, always came to earth at Christmas-tide to sing heavenly anthems for the Festa del Gesu Bambino, and to distribute blessings to those who were worthy.

Perhaps they had trod upon the ice outside, and had wet the soles of their slippers, so that they had been forced to set them up on end to dry. She had no doubt they would be gone in the morning.

The tremulous voice had ceased some time ago, and now the organ was sending forth deep, heavy chords that made the air thrill and vibrate. The pew in which Nina sat quite shook with the sounds, and she shrank away from the wooden back, and cuddled down upon the cushion in the seat, feeling very mysterious and awestruck, but withal quite warm and happily expectant.

"Ah, ah!" she thought, "they are coming, - the angels are coming. That is why the seat trembles so. There are so many of them that though they step very lightly it shakes the ground. He, up there, is playing their march music for them. Oh, I know! I know! I have seen the soldiers in the streets; and when they came one could feel the ground tremble, and they had music, too, - they kept step to it. I 'll lie very still and not move, and maybe I can even get a glimpse of the Gesu Bambino himself, and if I should - ah! *if* I should, then I know I 'd never be tired nor cold nor sad-hearted any more."

Nina started suddenly to her feet. The place was filled with a soft, white radiance. Faintly, as though from a distance, came the sounds of delicious music, and a rare fragrance was in all the air. What was it? Oh, what was it? She felt her heart beat louder and faster, and she thought she must cry out for very pain of its throbbing. But she made no sound, only waited and watched in breathless wonder and anticipation.

The light about her grew clearer and more lustrous; the faint strains of melody more glorious, and the perfumed air sweeter still; and lo! the whole place was thronged with white-winged spirits, clad all in garments so pure and spotless that they glistered at every turn. Each seemed to have in charge some precious treasure which she clasped lovingly to her breast, and all were so beautiful and tender-eyed that Nina could not be afraid. The dazzling forms flitted to and fro like filmy clouds; and as one passed very near her, Nina stretched out her hand to grasp her floating robe. But though she scarcely touched it, it was enough to make the delicate fabric sag and droop as if some strange weight had suddenly been attached to it. Its wearer paused in her flight, and glanced down at her garment anxiously, and then for an instant appeared to be trying to remember something. In her eyes there grew a troubled look, but she shook her head and murmured, -

"Alas! What have I done? What can I have done? I can think of no way in which I have let the world touch me, and yet I must have, for my robe is weighted, and - " But here she suddenly espied Nina.

"Ah!" she cried, her deep eyes clearing, "it was you, then, little mortal. For a moment I was struck with fear. You see if a bit of the world attaches to our garments it makes them heavy and weighs them down, and it is a long time ere they regain their lightness. Such a mishap seldom occurs, for generally we are only too glad to keep our minds on perfect things. But once in a long, long while we may give a thought to earth, and then it always hangs upon us like a clog; and if we did not immediately try to shake it off, we should soon be quite unable to rid ourselves of it, and it would grow and grow, and by and by we should have lost the power to rise above the earth, and should have to be poor worldlings like the rest; and, on the other hand, if the worldlings would only throw off all the earth-thoughts that weigh them down, they would become lighter and more spotless, and at last be one of us. But if it was you who touched my robe and if I can help you, I am not afraid. What do you wish, little one?"

For a moment Nina could find no voice in which to reply; but by and by she gained courage to falter out, -

"I came in here because I heard most beautiful music, and I thought it might be the Santa Maria singing to the Bambinetto, since it is his birthday - or will be to-morrow; and I thought - I did not mean to do wrong, but I thought maybe if I could see the Gesu Santissimo once, only once, I should never be tired nor cold nor sad-hearted any more. They say on the Festa del Gesu Bambino one gets most beautiful gifts. I have never got any gifts; but perhaps he might give me one if I promised to be very good and to take most excellent care of it and never to lose it."

By this time the whole company of spirits, seeing their

sister in conversation with a little mortal, had crowded eagerly about; and as Nina finished her sentence they all cried out in the sweetest, most musical chorus imaginable, -

"She wants a gift, - the earth-child wants a gift; and she promises to be very good, and to take excellent care of it and never lose it. The little one shall have a gift."

But most gently they were silenced by a nod from the spirit to whom Nina had first spoken.

"Dear child," she said, "we are the Christmas spirits, - Peace, Love, Hope, Good-will, and all the rest. We come from above, and we are laden with good gifts for mankind. To whomever is willing to receive we give; but, alas! so few care for what we bring. They misuse it or lose it; and that makes us very sad, for each gift we carry is most good and perfect."

"Oh! how can they?" cried Nina. "I would be so careful of mine, dear spirits. I would lock it away, and -"

But here the spirit interrupted her with a pitying smile and the words, -

"But you should never do that, dear one. If one shuts away one's gifts and does not let others profit by them, that is ill too. One must make the best of them, share them with the world always, and remember whence they come."

"Will you show me some of your gifts?" asked Nina, timidly.

The spirit drew nearer and took from her bosom a

glittering gem. It was clear and flawless, and though it was white a thousand sparks of lame broke from its heart, and flashed their different hues to every side. As Nina looked, wrapped in admiration, she felt her heart grow big, and she felt a great longing to do some one a kindness, - to do good to some one, no matter to whom.

The spirits gazed at her kindling eyes.

"There!" they cried in joyous unison, "Love has already given you her gift. The way you must use it is always to put in everything you do. It will never grow less, but will always grow more if you do as we say. And it is the same with Hope and Peace and Good-will and all the rest. If all to whom we give our gifts should use them aright, the world would hold a festival all the year."

And at this all the blessed throng closed about her, and loaded her down with their offerings, until she was quite overcome with gratitude and emotion.

"All we ask is that you use them well," they repeated with one accord. "Let nothing injure them, for some day you will be called to account for them all, you know. And now you are to have a special gift, - one by which you can gain world-praise and world-glory. And oh! be careful of it, dear; it will gain for you great good if you do not abuse it, and you need never be tired nor cold nor sad-hearted any more -"

"But I have no place to keep all these things," cried Nina. "I have no home. I live anywhere. I am only a poor little Italian singing-girl. I -"

"Keep them in your heart," answered the spirits, softly; and then one of them bent over and kissed her upon the lips.

"Ah, *gracia*, *gracia*, - thanks, thanks!" she cried; but even as she spoke she sank back in dismay, for everything about her was dark and still, and for a moment she did not know where she was. Then groping blindly about in the shadow, she felt the wooden back of the pew in which she sat, and then she remembered.

But the gifts, - the spirits' Christmas gifts to her. Where were they? For a long time she searched, stretching out her hand and passing it over cushion, bench, and floor; but all in vain. No heavenly object met her grasp, and at last she gave a poor little moan of disappointment and sorrow, -

"It was only a dream after all, - only a dream."

But now through the tall windows stole a faint streak of light. It grew ever stronger, and by its aid Nina made her way to the doors, in order to escape from the church in which she had slept away the night. But alas! they were closed and fastened tight. She could not get out. She wandered to and fro through the silent aisles, growing quite familiar with the dusky place and feeling not at all afraid. She thought over her dream, and recalled the fact that it was Christmas Day, - the Festa del Gesu Bambino.

"It was a dream," she mused; "but it was a beautiful one! Perhaps the spirits gave it to me for my Christmas gift. Perhaps the Gesu bade them give it me for my Christmas gift;" and just as a glorious burst of sunshine struck through the illuminated windows, she took up her little fiddle, raised her bow and her voice at the same time, and sang out in worshipful gratitude, -

"Mira, cuor mio durissimo,
Il bel Bambin Gesu,
Che in quel presepe asprissimo,
Or lo fai nascer tu!"

She did not hear a distant door open, nor did she see through it the man who had unconsciously lured her into the church the evening before by the power of his playing. No; she was conscious of nothing but her singing and the sweet, long notes she was drawing with her bow from the strings of her beloved violin.

But she did hear, after she had finished, a low exclamation, and then she did see that same man hastening toward her with outstretched hands.

"Child, child," he cried, "how came you here! And such a voice! *such* a voice! Why, it is a gift from Heaven!"

And amid all the excitement that followed, - the excitement of telling who she was and hearing that she was to be taken care of and given a home and trained to sing, - that, in fact, she was never to be tired nor cold nor sad-hearted any more, - she had time to think,

"Ah! *now* I know. It was not a dream; it was the truth. I have all my gifts in my heart for safe keeping. And my voice - hear! The player-man says it is a gift from Heaven. And oh, I will always use it with love and good-will, as the spirits bade me. They said it every one did so it would be a *festa* all the year."

Choose from Thousands of 1stWorldLibrary Classics By

Ada Leverson	Charles Ives	Evelyn Everett-green
Adolphus William Ward	Charles Kingsley	Everard Cotes
Aesop	Charles Klein	F. H. Cheley
Agatha Christie	Charles Lathrop Pack	F. J. Cross
Alexander Aaronsohn	Charles Whibley	Federick Austin Ogg
Alexander Kielland	Charles Willing Beale	Ferdinand Ossendowski
Alexandre Dumas	Charlotte M. Braeme	Francis Bacon
Alfred Gatty	Charlotte M. Yonge	Francis Darwin
Alfred Ollivant	Charlotte Perkins Stetson	Frances Hodgson Burnett
Alice Duer Miller	Clair W. Hayes	Frances Parkinson Keyes
Alice Turner Curtis	Clarence Day Jr.	Frank Gee Patchin
Alice Dunbar	Clarence E. Mulford	Frank Harris
Ambrose Bierce	Clemence Housman	Frank Jewett Mather
Amelia E. Barr	Confucius	Frank L. Packard
Andrew Lang	Cornelis DeWitt Wilcox	Frank V. Webster
Andrew McFarland Davis	Cyril Burleigh	Frederic Stewart Isham
Andy Adams	D. H. Lawrence	Frederick Trevor Hill
Anna Sewell	Daniel Defoe	Frederick Winslow Taylor
Annie Besant	David Garnett	Friedrich Kerst
Annie Hamilton Donnell	Don Carlos Janes	Friedrich Nietzsche
Annie Payson Call	Donald Keyhoe	Fyodor Dostoyevsky
Annonaymous	Dorothy Kilner	G.A. Henty
Anton Chekhov	Dougan Clark	G.K. Chesterton
Arnold Bennett	Douglas Fairbanks	Gabrielle E. Jackson
Arthur Conan Doyle	E. Nesbit	Garrett P. Serviss
Arthur M. Winfield	E.P.Roe	Gaston Leroux
Arthur Ransome	E. Phillips Oppenheim	George Ade
Atticus	Edgar Rice Burroughs	Geroge Bernard Shaw
B.H. Baden-Powell	Edith Van Dyne	George Durston
B. M. Bower	Edith Wharton	George Ebers
Baroness Emmuska Orczy	Edward J. O'Biren	George Eliot
Baroness Orczy	Edward S. Ellis	George MacDonald
Basil King	Edwin L. Arnold	George Meredith
Bayard Taylor	Eleanor Atkins	George Orwell
Ben Macomber	Eliot Gregory	George Tucker
Bertha Muzzy Bower	Elizabeth Gaskell	George W. Cable
Bjornstjerne Bjornson	Elizabeth McCracken	George Wharton James
Booth Tarkington	Elizabeth Von Arnim	Gertrude Atherton
Boyd Cable	Ellem Key	Grace E. King
Bram Stoker	Emerson Hough	Grace Gallatin
C. Collodi	Emily Dickinson	Grant Allen
C. E. Orr	Enid Bagnold	Guillermo A. Sherwell
C. M. Ingleby	Enilor Macartney Lane	Gulielma Zollinger
Carolyn Wells	Erasmus W. Jones	Gustav Flaubert
Catherine Parr Traill	Ernie Howard Pie	H. A. Cody
Charles A. Eastman	Ethel Turner	H. B. Irving
Charles Dickens	Ethel Watts Mumford	H.C. Bailey
Charles Dudley Warner	Eugenie Foa	H. G. Wells
Charles Farrar Browne	Eugene Wood	H. H. Munro

H. Irving Hancock
H. Rider Haggard
H. W. C. Davis
Hamilton Wright Mabie
Hans Christian Andersen
Harold Avery
Harold McGrath
Harriet Beecher Stowe
Harry Houidini
Helent Hunt Jackson
Helen Nicolay
Hendrik Conscience
Hendy David Thoreau
Henri Barbusse
Henrik Ibsen
Henry Adams
Henry Ford
Henry Frost
Henry James
Henry Jones Ford
Henry Seton Merriman
Henry W Longfellow
Herbert A. Giles
Herbert N. Casson
Herman Hesse
Homer
Honore De Balzac
Horace Walpole
Horatio Alger Jr.
Howard Pyle
Howard R. Garis
Hugh Lofting
Hugh Walpole
Humphry Ward
Ian Maclaren
Inez Haynes Gillmore
Irving Bacheller
Israel Abrahams
Ivan Turgenev
J.G.Austin
J. Henri Fabre
J. M. Barrie
J. Macdonald Oxley
J. S. Fletcher
J. S. Knowles
J. Storer Clouston
Jack London
Jacob Abbott
James Allen
James Andrews
James Baldwin

James DeMille
James Joyce
James Lane Allen
James Lane Allen
James Oliver Curwood
James Oppenheim
James Otis
James R. Driscoll
Jane Austen
Jens Peter Jacobsen
Jerome K. Jerome
John Burroughs
John Cournos
John F. Kennedy
John Gay
John Glasworthy
John Habberton
John Joy Bell
John Kendrick Bangs
John Milton
John Philip Sousa
Jonas Lauritz Idemil Lie
Jonathan Swift
Joseph A. Altsheler
Joseph Carey
Joseph Conrad
Joseph E. Badger Jr
Joseph Hergesheimer
Joscph Jacobs
Julian Hawthrone
Julies Vernes
Justin Huntly McCarthy
Kakuzo Okakura
Kenneth Grahame
Kenneth McGaffey
Kate Langley Bosher
Kate Langley Bosher
Katherine Cecil Thurston
Katherine Stokes
L. A. Abbot
L. T. Meade
L. Frank Baum
Latta Griswold
Laura Lee Hope
Laurence Housman
Leo Tolstoy
Leonid Andreyev
Lewis Carroll
Lilian Bell
Lloyd Osbourne
Louis Tracy

Louisa May Alcott
Lucy Fitch Perkins
Lucy Maud Montgomery
Lydia Miller Middleton
Lyndon Orr
M. Corvus
M. H. Adams
Margaret E. Sangster
Margaret Vandercook
Margret Penrose
Maria Edgeworth
Maria Thompson Daviess
Mariano Azuela
Marion Polk Angellotti
Mark Overton
Mark Twain
Mary Austin
Mary Catherine Crowley
Mary Cole
Mary Hastings Bradley
Mary Roberts Rinehart
Mary Rowlandson
M. Wollstonecraft Shelley
Maud Lindsay
Max Beerbohm
Myra Kelly
Nathaniel Hawthrone
Nicolo Machiavelli
O. F. Walton
Oscar Wilde
Owen Johnson
P.G. Wodehouse
Paul and Mabel Thorne
Paul G. Tomlinson
Paul Severing
Percy Brebner
Peter B. Kyne
Plato
R. Derby Holmes
R. L. Stevenson
R. S. Ball
Rabindranath Tagore
Rahul Alvares
Ralph Henry Barbour
Ralph Waldo Emmerson
Rene Descartes
Rex Beach
Rex E. Beach
Richard Harding Davis
Richard Jefferies
Richard Le Gallienne

Robert Barr
Robert Frost
Robert Gordon Anderson
Robert L. Drake
Robert Lansing
Robert Lynd
Robert Michael Ballantyne
Robert W. Chambers
Rosa Nouchette Carey
Rudyard Kipling
Samuel B. Allison
Samuel Hopkins Adams
Sarah Bernhardt
Selma Lagerlof
Sherwood Anderson
Sigmund Freud
Standish O'Grady
Stanley Weyman
Stella Benson
Stephen Crane
Stewart Edward White
Stijn Streuvels
Swami Abhedananda

Swami Parmananda
T. S. Ackland
T. S. Arthur
The Princess Der Ling
Thomas A. Janvier
Thomas A Kempis
Thomas Anderton
Thomas Bailey Aldrich
Thomas Bulfinch
Thomas De Quincey
Thomas H. Huxley
Thomas Hardy
Thomas More
Thornton W. Burgess
U. S. Grant
Valentine Williams
Various Authors
Victor Appleton
Virginia Woolf
Walter Camp
Walter Scott
Washington Irving
Wilbur Lawton

Wilkie Collins
Willa Cather
Willard F. Baker
William Dean Howells
William le Queux
W. Makepeace Thackeray
William W. Walter
Winston Churchill
Yei Theodora Ozaki
Yogi Ramacharaka
Young E. Allison
Zane Grey

www.ingramcontent.com/pod-product-compliance
Lightning Source LLC
Chambersburg PA
CBHW031851170626
46807CB00004B/1677